WYLDBLOOD

ISSUE 16

Wyldblood Magazine #16 - January 2025

Print ISBN-978-1-914417-20-7

Publisher: Wyldblood Press, Thicket View, Bakers Lane, Maidenhead SL6 6PX UK. www.wyldblood.com **Editor:** Mark Bilsborough. Single issues available worldwide via Amazon and from wyldblood.com/shop

Submissions: we are regularly open for submissions of flash fiction, short stories and novels – check our website for our current status and requirements. We are a paying market. We also need artwork, people to review us, and people to review *for* us. Email contact@wyldblood.com

Wyldblood 17 will be out in July 2025

Cover art by Rich Stahnke

Editorial

Mark Bilsborough

Welcome, and apologies for the longer than usual gap between issues. We're back with the usual mix of stories and comments, though once again reality is stranger than fiction so if you really want a dose of improbable storytelling I'd suggest watching the news.

This time around we've got fresh fiction from a roster or our Wyldblood favourites – all the authors in this issue have been published by us before (some many times) and most have a long list of publications in other fine places. For our longest piece this time. we've got **Jacey Bedford**, with her *Song of Unmaking* – a superpowers tale with tragic consequences. Jacey's a multi-published author with DAW – we're big fans of her Psi-Tec sci-fi and her engaging fantasy *The Amber Crown*, as well as Chairing the Milford Writers Workshop (more on that later).

We've got a rare SF story from successful crime novelist **Steve Burford** – *The Art of War* – delving between the blurred lines of what's real and what isn't. If you like what you see here check out his police-procedural *Crossed Lines* (and others) from NineStar Press or his fantasy novel *Moon King* from Dancing Unicorn.

We've got **Mark Rigney's** *Boggle Dog and Blue Cat* giving us more robot-based SF – you may remember Mark's fine *Dash Nine* stories from earlier Wyldbloods. Mark has plenty of great stories in places like Lightspeed but he's also written extensively for theatre and his words have been performed across the US and internationally.

Liam Hogan gives us another fine story – *Two Percent* – all about black holes and the prospects of surviving one. Check out Liam's extended short fiction *The Mortsafe* – in the Call of the Wyld collection, his award-winning stories in the *Best of British Science Fiction*, amongst other places, and his collections *Happy Ending NOT Guaranteed* from Arachne Press and *A Short History of the Future* out in March from NewCon Press.

We also have a new story from **Holley Cornetto,** who also wrote the very first story in the very first issue of Wyldblood Magazine. *Maiden of the Rock* is a fantasy story (yes, mermaids) and continues our tradition of thoughtful tales that challenge your assumptions. She's a creative writing teacher with a string of writing credits – check out her chilling novella *We Haunt These Woods* from Bleeding Edge Books.

Cardiff writer **JL George** gives us *Coblyn,* an unsettling fantasy horror. She's written for us a few times (including our favourite T*hawing* from #1), and for many other fine magazines. Check out her novel, *The Word,* from Parthian Books.

M Luke McDonell's *The Obscurists* rounds out our collection, a character-based sci-fi portal story with plenty of action. We published her first in issue #12 with her fine story *The Leisure Class* and we've been lucky enough to see a sneak preview of her novel-length material which will blow you away when she publishes it. Check out her other work in places like Shoreline of Infinity and track down her excellent *SF in SF* podcast.

I wanted to highlight a couple of non-Wyldblood things for writers that might be of interest. I manage a group of **online novel writing groups** for the British Science Fiction Association (BSFA). These 'Orbit' groups usually have five members and critique on a bi-monthly schedule – each member sends in a novel chunk (usually 10-15,000 words) and gets feedback from the rest of the group – a sort of beta readers+ setup. The groups are free for BSFA members and, like the BSFA itself, are open to anyone, whatever their nationality or country of residence. The BSFA also runs short story workshop groups. If you're interested, check out the BSFA's website (www.bsfa.co.uk) or email me direct at orbitnovels@bsfa.co.uk

The **Milford Writers Workshop** is open to anyone with a paid-sales writing credit to their name and runs twice a year (once as a workshop, once as a retreat) in the glorious Gladstone Library in North Wales. You may have heard of the Milford critiquing method – that's where it started way back in the 1950s when Damon Knight and James Blish kicked things off. Milford's seen an impressive roster of attendees in the past (check out their website www.milfordsf.co.uk for the full rogues gallery) and there's always a mix of high profile, experienced writers and newer talent. It also runs a bursary scheme and is open to anyone, from anywhere. At the time of publication there were still places available for their September workshop.

As for our future plans, well, we'll be publishing more than in 2024 (when we followed the MCU's fairly dismal lead with only one major offering) but we're moving away from our (ahem) quarterly schedule to something more manageable, given our time and resources. Expect our next regular issue in July. We'll also be revamping the look and format of the magazine from #17 onwards so it's more in line with the 'anthology paperback' style that's been trending in our part of the publishing industry. We'll finally get around to publishing a few novellas too (maybe something longer) and, yes, there'll be more new flash fiction on our website. Wyldblood t-shirts too (not even kidding).

That's all for now – enjoy the stories.

Mark

Boggle Dog and Blue Cat

Mark Rigney

Kim spotted them first.

"Uncle Brody!" he cried, though I wasn't his uncle. Kim had no living relatives so far as anyone knew.

"Hey!" he called again, as he ran crossways over the field, dodging our ripening melons, our endless trailing cucumbers. "I got news, real news! There's a Boggle Dog comin' up the road! A Boggle Dog *and* a Blue Cat!"

We had a few dozen field hands out that morning, each one of us hell-bent on reviving the former glory of Indiana's "melon alley," but Kim ran straight toward me, hopscotching the vines and ignoring everyone else under the assumption I'd be most likely to believe him—which I didn't. A Boggle Dog? Up and moving around?

"Not possible," I said, once Kim, still jabbering, got close enough that I could hear him sweat. Boggle Dogs, Blue Cats, and pretty much every other play-bot had long ago been plundered for spare parts, fodder to make or maintain something more essential.

Not that Kim was giving up. A teen on a mission, he flung an arm out and up, toward the merciless sun. "Brody, you think I'd run this far, in this heat, just for a *joke*?"

"You?" I said. "Never." By which I meant that we both knew he had a well-deserved reputation as the most unreliable of sentries, the bored kid who cries wolf. My fellow Outposters had every reason to believe that I was about to become the credulous victim of his latest unfunny prank.

Kim, stung, caught the others exchanging eye-rolls. He said, faltering, "Brody, I ain't kidding."

"C'mon," I said, as I cinched my belt and reflexively patted my sidearm, snug in its holster. "Show me."

As we topped the last low rise and looked down on the still-smooth ribbon of Highway 41, I saw what Kim had claimed: a great brown-and-white mop of a Boggle Dog, shuffling and cavorting its way down the otherwise deserted southbound lanes, while beside it paced a Blue Cat, tail held high, as regal and sedate as any Nile-born goddess.

"See?" said Kim. "Told ya'."

If a jet airplane had landed, fully functional and loaded with passengers from our not-so-distant but absolutely unrecoverable past, I could not have been more dumb-founded. How had these two bots survived the past two decades, when so much had been lost, destroyed? The Blue Cat, especially, looked as if it had just stepped through the cellophane front of its original packaging.

"I found 'em first." Kim's expression was conniving, hopeful. "Does that mean I can have 'em?"

"You know better," I said, and I set off downslope, my boots puffing dust in the rain-starved midsummer dirt. In this sector, the cucumbers, and even some of the melons, were clearly ready for a first harvest. I made a mental note to rotate field hands this way next morning.

"Hey!" cried Kim, realizing that if he didn't scamper, I'd be first to greet our new and fantastic arrivals. "Wait for me!"

Boggle Dog started causing trouble before I'd even escorted the two bots back to the Outpost, first by getting fabulously muddy in a roadside ditch, then by planting his oven-mitt paws on the shoulders of one of our youngest members and knocking the poor girl flat. Of course, she was carrying a pail of chicken feed; of course, it spilled.

"Whoops!" Boggle Dog barked, his furry, good-natured face just inches from that of his wriggling victim. "Just trying to be friendly. Here, let me help you up."

Which, of course, the bot couldn't manage.

"Boggle Dog," said Blue Cat, ever patient. "You're making bad decisions. Again."

Kim dusted the girl off, but he was looking at me, questions tugging his mouth half-open.

"Par for the course," I said, a metaphor I wasn't sure that Kim, growing up in a world without golf, would understand. The bottom line: it was in Boggle Dog's nature to make bad decisions. That was how he'd been since his very first appearance, in the eponymous children's book, *Boggle Dog and Blue Cat*, and then on through the spin-off animated series (all six seasons), and finally, just before the collapse—and I'm talking here about the collapse of pretty much everything—in their ultimate iteration as that year's hottest holiday toy, the life-size, interactive play-bots that now stood before us. Kim knew them only through the book. We had a copy in our modest library, its pages stained with drool and dirty fingerprints.

Another hundred meters brought us to the Outpost proper, a scatter of unlike buildings crouching just beyond easy view of the highway. New Patoka is the name others use—the far-flung, allies in the region—but we just call it the Outpost. Nationwide, there must be thousands like it, and none of any great size.

Given the hour, the only folks around were the elderly, a few child-minders, and the youngest kids, the ones who couldn't be trusted to complete even a simple, menial task, but those who were on hand could barely keep their eyes in their heads.

"Brody," said ancient, arthritic Merton, pointing a knuckle-boned finger at Boggle Dog. "Why are you bringing trouble like that?"

Before I could answer, around the corner came Shayna Maxwell-Jones, newly rotated from metalwork to child-care. She kept a toddler gripped in each strong hand, but when she saw Blue Cat, her eyes flew wide and she let go of both kids. One hand clapped itself over her mouth.

With well-mannered, effortless poise, Blue Cat said, still facing Merton, "I beg to differ. I am not trouble. I am Blue Cat. And this is the one and only Boggle Dog."

Too late, I remembered; too late, I tried to shush Blue Cat. No good, no use. At the sound of Blue Cat's voice, Shayna fainted, listing sideways as if she'd been shot.

"I," said Blue Cat, with a critical gaze, "had nothing to do with that."

But she did. She had everything to do with it.

The meeting that night began as our meetings always do, with an acknowledgment of the three civilizations that came before us, the Mississippians, the Shawnee, and the United States. Boggle Dog and Blue Cat had been instructed not to attend. While we decided their fate, they would remain in Merton's back yard. The rest of us were present, even the little ones, lolling into dreamland in their parents' laps or struggling against sleep as if out of habit, and we spilled across the baseball diamond's bleachers and onto the infield, forming a rough circle around home plate. We still played the odd game, now and then, though we'd long since run out of decent balls.

The battle lines were drawn early. There were those in favor of scuttling Boggle Dog and Blue Cat for parts, or maybe selling them whole to what tech gurus remained over in Bloomington, but others wanted to keep them intact, as playthings for our children. All these options made sense—we needed the bots' sensory apparatus, working microchips, and small-scale hydraulics, but then, we also needed frivolity and distraction, and we had precious little of either one—so of course the meeting ran long, and Sam Dixon claimed that if we harvested the two bots' solar collectors, we could run a laptop on steady voltage twelve hours straight—he said it would be almost like we were plugged into the 'net again—and then voices rose and tempers frayed and we damn near turned into a flock of starlings, quarrelling over stubble in a late-fall field. But, at last, at ten thirty-seven, a vote was called, because that's how we solve dilemmas here at the Outpost, by popular vote, as defined by our adaptation of Robert's immortal, damnable Rules.

Except that in this case, no one wanted to be the first to raise a hand, not before checking with Shayna.

She stood to one side, anchored by an elbow to the bleachers as if they were all that prevented her from taking to her heels. Painfully aware of our focused good will, she kept her gaze on the soft, dusty ground and said, "You all know I only got one way to vote. Only one way I *can* vote. That don't mean you should be followin' my lead."

I glanced at Kim, who hovered near the backstop, fidgeting like mad. He'd rehearsed an impassioned, surprisingly cogent speech on the bots' behalf, but then hadn't had the courage to deliver it.

Fenella Jimenez, who ran all our meetings, let her gavel rap once on the upside-down Sterling Super Bru beer crate that doubled as desk and lectern. The wooden slats shivered from the blow, threatening to fly apart, dissolve.

"One more time, people," Fenella called out, as if she wanted the whole Patoka watershed to hear. "The vote is to keep Boggle Dog and Blue Cat here with us, intact and interactive. If we vote against, we'll have a second vote to decide what exactly to do with them. So. All in favor, say 'Aye.'"

Again, everyone fixed on Shayna, but after the briefest hesitation, a good three quarters of our number raised their hands and murmured, "Aye," and a few even shouted, as if they were in church, testifying. At last Shayna, more quietly, said the same, and Kim, ecstatic, did a crazy, frenetic jig.

"Right," said Fenella. "A clear majority, so. The bots stay. Meeting adjourned, let's get some rest."

Kim raced off, eager, I knew, to break the news. I let him go, and worked my way toward Shayna. She was surrounded by a knot of well-wishers as if she were the bereaved at a funeral, in need of comfort. One by one, they reached out, lightly touching her elbows, her shoulders. Some offered hugs. I joined this shambolic receiving line, and when it was my turn, I said, "Listen, Shayna, I know I'm the one that brought them in, but if it gets to be too much, well, I can do whatever needs doing."

She gave her head a quick shake, eyes diamond-bright. I guess some tears never quite fall. "I know it's not Momma," she said. "Not really."

I agreed with a shrug. "Processors. A recording."

"It's a ghost," said Shayna, sounding defeated. "A haunting."

Given my status as an Artisan, by which we meant Expert, by which we meant "best available and sadly lacking," I only rotated off field duty once every two weeks, and then only for a single day. I'd grown up with gardens, and at the Outpost, I'd learned on the fly how to scale up and delegate. Back in the COVID days, I would have been labeled an "essential worker."

Our crops generally took me far from the Outpost, sometimes miles away, leaving a long trudge home come sunset, so I didn't see much of Boggle Dog or Blue Cat for a while. When we did cross paths, in early summer sunlight, pearly and muggy and thick, or sometimes at night, with the clouds still lit but the land going dark, Kim was always on hand, Kim and a gaggle of small fry. He'd always disdained child-minding, pouting whenever that rotation became unavoidable, but now he relished his role as ringleader and de facto parent of two pets.

More often than not, I'd spot Shayna loitering at the edge of the gang, hanging with an addict's naked, strained desire on every syllable Blue Cat uttered. Bkue Cat seemed aware that she had caught Shayna's attention, and often cast sly, feline glances Shayna's way, as if sizing her up—which she wasn't, of course. Why on earth should Blue Cat have been programmed to know the identity of Shayna's long-dead mother, the human who'd provided her signature voice?

Kim couldn't be with the bots all the time, which was a problem, because Boggle Dog really did make bad decisions. Constantly. True, he took his fair share of naps to recharge, and he generally slept through the night, but his waking hours were an endless hullabaloo of pratfalls and disasters. Most were minor, like walking into a wall nose-first, or trying his level best to eat a downspout, but he also got in with the chickens (and nearly killed one before it reared and flew at him, talons up), and in another instance, he tore Fenella's best (and only) eiderdown pillow into shredded, irreparable pieces.

"It's not his fault," said Kim, feet planted wide to beat back any dissent. "He's just being himself."

The really galling thing was that Blue Cat didn't serve as a deterrent. Time and time again, Boggle Dog would propose an inane, mutton-headed plan, and rather than put her foot down, Blue Cat would shake her queenly head and offer a tolerant, resigned purr. "Oh, Boggle Dog. You're making a very bad decision."

It must have seemed like a charming dynamic to the programmers who, back in the final hey-day of high tech civilization, had all the tools required to make a reality of their favorite "educational" toy, but to my way of thinking, they completely negated the instructive aspects of the book. In those old paper pages, or even the TV shows, the fallout of Boggle Dog's choices could be evaluated at a safe remove, with no physical repercussions. Once actualized, however, the legions of A.I. Boggle Dogs did real damage. My memories of how business oversight used to work are hazy, but I'm pretty certain that if the world hadn't gone belly-up a few months after the introduction of the Boggle Dog and Blue Cat play-bots, they would have been recalled. Permanently.

Five nights after the bots' arrival, Shayna crept in with me, something she hadn't done for six months or more. I thought she'd gotten over me, over her need for someone much older than herself to supervise her goals and soothe her fears. Like Kim—like most of us, really—she'd lost her entire family. For some, that's a pill you can learn to swallow. For Shayna, abandonment, however unintentional, had been devastating.

Despite the many times she'd joined me in my bed (barely private, and definitely built for one), we'd only made love, if you could call it that, a grand total of twice. True, we were visually striking—I'm Scotch-Irish and prone to peeling sunburns, while Shayna is richly brown, like a fine walnut plank—but as lovers, we'd been a poor match. She was needy, furtive, hurried. It was like she wanted to claw something out of me, something neither of us could name or provide. For my part, I was old enough that I wanted it slow and relaxed or not at all. I never minded her presence, though, and I never turned her away. The world being what it was, I felt, even in those days, a kind of duty to provide what comfort I could.

On that night, she appeared in the doorway, one shadow among a thousand, and she whispered, "Brody?" which in shorthand meant, *Do you mind*? and I rolled over and made room in the dark, letting that soft rustle do my talking for me. She squeezed in, her back to me, and I draped what I hoped was a comforting arm. She said, "Kim's the one that got the whole story, but it sounds like those bots were living on some sort of estate up in Brown County. Their people been gone for years, and the bots didn't mind too much, but then there was a lightning strike, and a big fire, and I guess they hit the road."

I said, as gently as I could manage, "Did you explain?"

She shook her head, floating toward sleep. "Every time I work up the courage, I can't decide what to say."

Two days later, I was back in the north fields, leading the assault on an infestation of cucumber beetles. Pretty little things, those beetles, black and yellow like wasps, but with lengthwise stripes. We had no access to insecticides—we wouldn't have used them if we did—and now our plants were wilting, the results (so I read) of a bacterial infection spread by the beetles. The best we could dream up was to sweep the plants with brooms, knocking the beetles off the leaves and then smashing as many as possible. It was slow, frustrating work. It turns out that five acres of cucumber plants, even interspersed with watermelons, hold an infinite number of hungry beetles.

Highway 41 trailed along beside us as we worked, its deserted concrete arteries shimmering in the heat. The shoulders hadn't been mown in twenty years, maybe longer, and all that new growth made it hard to see the pavement anywhere close by, but from our position on the slope, we had a decent view, and it was while I was wiping sweat, adjusting my sun hat, and wishing to holy hell that nature had never invented either cucumbers or beetles that I heard the puttering sounds of an approaching engine. What marauding gangs there'd been had mostly self-destructed long ago, but I was intrigued, so I stood tall, shaded my eyes, and spotted a motorcycle headed our way, southbound. It flew a courier's pennant, and even at a distance, I recognized the crazy Mohawk helmet of one of our regulars on the Chambana run, Lester Bynes. That was a good sight to see. Lester's arrival meant saddlebags stuffed with news, mail, surprises.

But then Boggle Dog raced out of the weeds, all but leaping into the motorcycle's path. Lester swerved hard; the bike skidded. A moan of dismay went up from my co-workers—I wasn't the only one alert to Lester's arrival—a cry that rose into outright alarm as Lester's bike careened into the ditch. Lost from view, the motor sputtered like an old firework before going silent.

I cursed, threw down my broom, and ran for the spot where Lester had vanished. Boggle Dog, pursued now by Blue Cat, barked and pranced as if he'd just hit a home run.

Skin-and-bones Lester had a banged-up knee and a sprained wrist, and at first, he was too flustered to be mad. Later, once he'd been patched up by our tongue-clucking medics and realized he'd been run off the road by a toy, he was fit to be tied.

"Get rid of it!" he cried. "Take it apart, bolt by bolt!"

For the next several days, while Lester healed up, Boggle Dog and Blue Cat were exiled to an outlying barn, along with Kim, disgraced by default. That he got out of other work calls might have been some compensation, but dealing with Boggle Dog all by himself held less appeal by the hour.

Not that he was completely alone. Shayna joined the trio on their second night at the barn, and after trying unsuccessfully to engage Blue Cat in conversation, she settled for the next best thing: she talked, leaving Blue Cat to listen. Kim listened, too, although he kept nodding off, because it was late and the days were hot and long, and of course Shayna had a great deal to say, and I know all this because Shayna told me the whole tale, a few nights later, having sidled once more into my bed, fresh tears at the ready.

"I told that cat everything," Shayna said. "It was like I couldn't shut up."

To me, because I'd heard her story before, and because it seemed to encapsulate so many of the broken histories of my fellow Outposters, the journey of Shayna's mother verged on the mythological. Twenty years back, when Shayna was in grade school and the world was what then passed for normal, Joelle Maxwell-Jones, newly divorced and freshly ambitious, left her girls with her mother and abandoned Terre Haute in favor of Los Angeles, where she was certain that some form of stardom awaited. She had the looks, as Shayna always insisted (and she did; I'd seen pictures), and she had the voice—but then so, too, did a thousand others, and Hollywood's gates resisted her advances like a sea wall turning back breakers. But, instead of running for home, Joelle slipped into the world of voice-overs, first in commercials, then in computer gaming. From there, it was a hop, skip, and a jump to "the offer of a lifetime," the chance to be the voice of the one and only Blue Cat.

"She recorded on that project for six months," Shayna told me, back when we'd first become friends. "Six days a week. Little sounds, like sighs. Single words. Whole sentences, dialogue. They told her, 'We want Blue Cat to have self-possession. Strength. We want her to embody a strong, black woman.' And that's what my Momma gave."

As for Boggle Dog, he was voiced by a shaggy, endlessly enthusiastic surfer who went by the stage name of Johnny Vermont. According to Shayna, Johnny and Joelle got along famously, evidence that yes, sometimes, opposites attract.

Did Blue Cat experience the slightest pang of empathy as Shayna related how, on the heels of those six months, offers of steady work began flooding in? Did Blue Cat note the irony of how Joelle reached the pinnacle of her profession just as the collapse hit? There she was, in Los Angeles, with Shayna and her sister in Terre Haute. The miles between might as well have measured in the millions. They never saw each other again.

So, Blue Cat had listened to all that Shayna said, and when she was done, when even Kim had huddled into himself, his face safely to the wall, Blue Cat said, "Shayna. You have just related a very long and involved story."

Repeating that impervious, mechanical response sent Shayna right over the edge. How, she demanded of me, between bouts of choking sobs, could anything sound so much like her mother and still be so cold?

It occurred to me to ask how a warm, loving mother could have put two thousand miles between herself and her youngest child, but I held my tongue. Instead, I twisted the too-tight band of my wedding ring, and wondered for the umpteenth time what had become of my wife.

Despite her protestations that she would never go near Blue Cat again, it took only a day for Shayna to recover—or, as she put it to me, sheepishly, to weaken. There was no need to apologize. I understood.

And so, day after day, Boggle Dog carried right on making bad decisions. He punched holes in three screen doors; he dug up a bees' nest, scattering angry drones in all directions; he chased after Lester as he motored out of town; he lay down in the main kitchen doorway, and refused to move for an hour, forcing cooks and servers to step over him as if he were a corpse. The Outpost's various offspring still giggled, of course—what child doesn't delight in obvious misbehavior?—but for the rest of us, the act was getting old.

"Oh, Boggle Dog," said Blue Cat, in Joelle's matchless, long-suffering voice. "You are making very bad decisions."

Then came July 27th, and Boggle Dog's worst decision. That hound was up so early in the morning that he beat my crew to the fields by a good twenty minutes, and by the time we arrived, he'd crushed at least two hundred ripe fruit, leaving a trail of seedy, green cucumber pulp, all interspersed with the red-pink blood of smashed watermelon. He destroyed at least another hundred as we chased him, all hands on deck, and there went Boggle Dog barking and gamboling through our crop as if nothing could be more exhilarating, and there went the rest of us, shouting and pointing, making failed diving tackles, anything to stop that idiot bot from wiping out our food supply.

When we finally got him pinned, he lolled his tongue and licked the nearest face and panted. "Wasn't that fun? When can we do it again?"

I was winded, my hands on my knees, and Blue Cat sidled up behind me, too little, too late. For once, as if sensing the gravity of the situation, she sounded stern. "Boggle Dog," she muttered, "this was a *very* bad decision."

The meeting that night started early and didn't last a full thirty minutes. Merton reminded us that we were already low on stores for winter, also on goods to trade. Nancy Kicklighter provided a similarly bleak treasurer's report, one that took Boggle Dog's various desecrations into account. Sam Dixon harped again about what the bots' internal workings could do for our community, and then Kim spoke, which no one was expecting.

"I know Boggle Dog has to go," he said, in a quavering voice, "but Blue Cat—she's done no harm. And it's not her fault that Boggle Dog is programmed to be stupid."

When the vote came, no one raised their hand faster than me, and it turned out to be unanimous, a first for us. Blue Cat would be spared, but Boggle Dog would be deactivated, at once. Kim, thinking he would be named as executioner, was eyeing my gun sidelong when Sam clapped a hand to his shoulder and shook his head. "Too many parts we don't want to wreck. Sorry to deep-six your *Old Yeller* fantasies, but don't worry. You'll have a part to play."

Relieved but also, in a way, disappointed, Kim blinked rapidly and looked to me. "What," he demanded, "is an 'old yellow fantasy'?"

The fact was, disabling Boggle Dog posed a number of challenges. Inducing a short circuit could damage innumerable sensitive parts, as might an injection of equally incapacitating liquid insulators. In the end, we settled on light deprivation. We would trap Boggle Dog somewhere lightproof, then sit back and wait until the last of his battery cells ran dry.

Sam and two of his engineers spent a few hours modifying a dysfunctional freezer bay that had once belonged to a Panera restaurant, and the next morning, Kim lured Boggle Dog inside it. It was simplicity itself: all Kim had to say was that jumping into the freezer would be a monumentally bad choice, and quick as you please, Boggle Dog did exactly that.

"Wait!" cried Blue Cat, as Kim reached for the door. "Boggle Dog! That is *not* a good decision!"

Too late. Kim slammed the freezer shut, and just as it came to, I caught a final glimpse of Boggle Dog's trusting face, curious as ever, and looking pleased as punch with his latest misdeed.

It took longer than expected for Boggle Dog's battery to fail, and in the meantime (hours), we had to endure his heroic, muffled efforts to escape that freezer. He made endless plaintive, eager promises to be, in future, as good as gold and to never make bad decisions again. We did our best to stay out of earshot. Kim, agonizing over his duplicity, fled all the way to the river bottoms and stayed there until dusk.

Only Blue Cat, loyal to the end, stayed by that makeshift prison, and only when Boggle Dog's battery finally gave up the ghost did she end her vigil—and from that moment on, she also stopped talking.

At first, it seemed like a temporary programming choice: mourning a loved one, Blue Cat had been designed to be sullen, passive aggressive. The thing was, it lasted. Without her boon companion, she went mute and stayed that way.

Shayna was devastated. Against all odds, her mother had been resurrected, and now, for a second time, she'd been stolen away.

Nor did Blue Cat have the decency to ingratiate herself, to accept at last her status as a plaything. Instead, as Sam and his team began the delicate process of disassembling Boggle Dog, Blue Cat took to avoiding our children while never quite abandoning the Outpost. Over the ensuing week, we kept finding her in unexpected corners, mooning around, tail limp, head bowed, until at last, Shayna could stand it no longer. Early one morning, she woke me and pulled my sidearm from its holster. As I blinked at her, muzzy with sleep, she tapped the pistol grip and said, "Brody. I can't shoot my mother without help."

I nodded, rose, and dressed. I let Shayna carry the gun until we found Blue Cat, lurking around the machine shop, and then I took over. Before Shayna could change her mind, I put a single lethal bullet through Blue Cat's perfect head.

The impact knocked Blue Cat sideways, but then she shook herself and raised her eyes to ours. A wisp of smoke rose from the hole in her temple, making her look like a candle when the flame is blown out. Slowly, her voice garbled and metallic, she said, "No regrets."

I swallowed nervously, wondering at the long-dead programmer who'd for some capricious reason given Blue Cat those particular words to cap her existence. Or perhaps it had been Joelle, insisting on one final justification for all she'd left behind.

Later that night, Shayna lay curled against me, fresh from our first-ever round of mutually satisfying sex, and I said to her, surprising even myself, "It's okay. You're safe now."

By which I meant, *You're safe here with me.* By which I meant, I hope, that I would give what I had, and more, if possible, and that I would go on giving until I, too, spoke final words and gave myself over to whatever comes next, and that I would own my worst decisions together with my best, and that if she, Shayna, was willing, we might consider, down the road, adopting a teen named Kim, who didn't really have anything, but maybe had a future.

I wanted so desperately to communicate all this to Shayna, to say it aloud, to make that good decision, but I didn't trust my voice.

***Mark Rigney** has had over fifty short pieces find print in a gentle arc covering the last two decades, with stories in Lightspeed, Realms of Fantasy, and more. Theatrical credits, too, with play across the U.S., including off-Broadway, along with Canada, Hong Kong, Nepal, and Australia.*

Two Percent

Liam Hogan

"Here goes nothing!"

Connor's wiry arms are rigid with tension, his gaunt face wears death's grin as he plunges the *Naglfar* towards the gaping maw of a black hole maelstrom.

The theory connecting wormholes with singularities dates from the earliest days of Post-Einstein cosmology. We've always known that, if we were ever to investigate one as more than a textbook possibility, we'd need to find a strongly rotating black hole, as otherwise the only way to reach any wormhole it concealed would be via the event horizon. Even school kids know how that turns out. *Badly*. A one-way trip to oblivion.

But, somehow, against reason and against experience, we expected both black holes and their wormholes to be well behaved, sharply defined, like something out of a mathematical model, an *idealised* simulation.

A strange, warbling sound fills our cabin as the *Naglfar* shakes, as the communications antenna that juts proud from her nose glows fiery red, then incandescent white, before flaring into non-existence. It takes a long, terrifying moment to realise I'm the one making the animalistic noises, as I press myself deep into the rattling bucket seat and chaos erupts on the forward screens. Savage reality overtaking neat theory; the event horizon of a rotating black hole is as beset by storms as any planet with an atmosphere, as any gas giant whose hurricanes rage for centuries, or even as the surface of the sun, broiling with prominences and mass ejections, capable of lashing out at nearby planets and woe betide those without the protective shield of a magnetosphere. Singularities are as turbulent as any gas or liquid that spins and, in spinning, forms eddies and whirls, regions of different pressure and temperature, different potentials to rub against each other, energies building until they grow too potent to be contained. Black hole storms are as huge and powerful and *violent* as anything we could possibly have imagined, making even the monstrous solar flares of 2035, that turned the night skies into other-worldly rainbows as far south as the Mediterranean and briefly plunged the Earth back to the dark ages, look like a pretty good day for a picnic.

Five minutes; that's how long this particular storm will last, for us, anyway, assuming we survive the ride. Fifteen seconds in and those five minutes might as well be a millennia. We've been getting closer and closer to the black hole for the best part of a sol year, ever since waving our goodbyes to the *Einstein,* the gigantic interstellar science vessel that both birthed and named us. And, in five hectic minutes, we would either be smeared across some abstract physical barrier, or we'd be through and beyond, to who knows what and who knows where.

Those are the only two options but they sure as hell aren't *equal*. The *Einstein*'s formidable computers give us a generous two percent chance of navigating intact to the eye of the giant storm, the one relatively quiet area at the singularity's cataclysmic heart. After that, beyond the point where our limited physics apply, they refuse to hazard even an educated guess.

We were never supposed to get this close. Connor and I, we aren't what you would call proper scientists. Connor is the best pilot aboard the *Einstein,* thankfully, if rather prickly with it. Which probably explains why *I'm* the all-purpose engineer and second member of the two person team. I tolerate Connor because the one good thing you could say about his rampant misanthropy is that it's all encompassing, applying equally regardless of race or gender.

Doesn't make him any easier to live or work with, especially in the cramped confines of our exploratory craft. It just means I didn't take it as personally as others seem to. Right now, he's my only chance of surviving this messed up mission, and I, I suppose, his.

The problem with gravity wells is it can be just as hard to get into them as out. You might think it would be easy to fly into the sun, because all you need to do is keep on falling. It's not. Gravity tugs you faster and faster, potential energy becoming kinetic, and before you know it you've unwittingly reached orbital velocity. To get close, *really* close, close enough to spend time studying such a super-massive object, you have to somehow kill your speed; shed your kinetic energy and keep shedding it, the closer you want to get.

Which is *fine,* if you have a couple of stupendously powerful fusion engines and enough mass to eject, and if everything goes gloriously to plan. That is, until you're as close as anybody has ever been to a black hole, ready to deploy the squadron of science probes, to sit back and map the mind-bending monstrosity before beating a hasty retreat, and it's then that you--that is, *we*--realise there's a problem. An insolvable, impossible problem. A problem as massive as the black hole beneath our feet.

The engines that have been pushing against our orbital acceleration have degraded more than expected, much more than the sensors show. Which means we don't have enough *oomph* to get back out of the hole we've dug for ourselves. We've slammed the prison door behind us, and thrown away the key.

High, high above us, safely beyond the inexorable pull of the black hole, the science vessel listened dispassionately to our plight, and torpedoed our increasingly desperate suggestions. Sending another crewed mission was a no-no. Even if the *Einstein* could have manufactured another *Naglfar* in time, they wouldn't launch it until they'd worked out what went wrong with the propulsion system on ours. And the best way to do that (it seems) is to take our engines apart. Not much help to us. Sending a drone with extra fuel *appears* a better option, until they worked out just how impossible it is to match trajectories--especially since a drone would be using the same suspect engine technology. The *Naglfar* is already the smallest ship conceivable for our task, designed and constructed for just two people, so there's nothing we can do to lighten the load, other than to launch the science probes that have already been factored in to the equations. And no, before you ask, there's no escape pod. (No paddle, and no parachute.) Even if there was, it's no easier for a pod to reach escape velocity than for the *Naglfar*.

"If you can achieve a sharp enough elliptical orbit," Professor Elena Japoski said, a couple of hours back now, the image swimming in treacle as our AI manipulated the frame rate to compensate for our speed and the all too steep gravity well, "Then we might be able to pick up the *Naglfar* at the apogee. But to achieve such an orbit, you're going to have to get closer to the black hole. A *lot* closer."

"How much closer?" I asked, but damn if I hadn't already guessed I wasn't going to like the answer.

"*Very* close. The best plan we have," she went on, staring through the screen and a million miles of charged static, "is *through*."

"Through? Through *what*?" Connor scowled, rolling his eyes. Why couldn't scientists talk sense?

"*Through* the black hole. Or, more accurately the wormhole we believe lies behind the eye of the persistent storm you've mapped on its surface. Slingshotting the black hole's equatorial bulge, targeting the only region that appears calm enough to do so. Hitting the anomaly at a shallow enough angle, we think you won't actually *penetrate* the wormhole, just steal some of its rotational energy as you skip off."

"You *think?*"

"We are still searching for alternative solutions."

Code for there aren't any and we don't much fancy your chances.

"Though, in rather more positive news," she went on, the skin around her eyes crinkling, "since you'll be passing closer than we could possibly have hoped to both the black hole and the anomaly, there's some science--"

"Ah *nuts* to that," Connor snarled as he snapped the long range comms off.

"That's gonna come up in your next review," I joked, feeling sick to my stomach.

But, much as we crunched the numbers and racked our brains--what limited grey matter we had and those supposedly superior specimens on the science ship, the AI's quantum-neurons included--no better options presented. And the clock is ticking. Being this close to a black hole isn't healthy, not for long, no matter how much shielding you have. A black hole like this one is where some of the worst kinds of cosmic radiation originate. By now, or ideally a week ago if things had gone anything like to plan, we should have begun the long, slow climb back to the *Einstein,* should be escaping the radiation the singularity is spewing out. Instead, each time we spin giddily around the soul-wrenching impossibility, each time the staring black eye of the vortex looms into view, I wonder how long we could, or should, put the closest thing we had to an escape plan off, even if our chances make it akin to suicide. But then so is doing nothing, just slower, more certain, and ultimately (probably?) more painful. If we're hoping the probes return anything useful before each of them gets fried, we've so far been disappointed, though the scientists seem unbearably happy with the readings.

All they offer us guinea pigs is the supposed safest possible approach route. Somewhat like advising us not to step on the paving stone cracks as we pass through a den of hungry lions, crashing cymbals, Connor and I dressed in suits of raw meat.

I glance to my side, neck protesting the effort, the vibration and acceleration of the world's worst fairground ride. Something flies between us, hitting the back of the cabin with a sharp clatter despite all the other noise, despite the time and effort spent lashing everything we could down. Connor turns just his reddened, bulging eyes to me, the intense g-force making his expression impossible to read. The *Naglfar* pitches forward into an even steeper dive and *then...*

If I tell you it is impossible to describe what we experienced, then that is nothing more than the bare truth. But if I fail to at least *attempt* a description, you will suspect a ruse, a fake, a fiction, so even though my words, anyone's words, can never be enough, (and pray god no-one else suffers the same experience), I will try my best.

The vertigo you feel while stood beneath a tall building, looking up as clouds race by, is nothing to the sensation of staring straight down the throat of that vortex. A black hole is not, on the whole, very black, not as matter tears itself violently apart on its fringes, half to be consumed, half energetically spewed out. But the centre of that rotating eye is as utterly black as anything could ever be, made all the darker by flashes and flickers of energies just beyond visible at its edges, lightning that behaves almost like water swirling around a plughole, the sense that with the mightiest engines in all of creation, we are being sucked into the abyss, and there's no return. And even if we *did* have those engines, and if we threw them into desperate reverse, that would seal our fate and destroy us, stealing the very speed we need to escape. Instead, we're plunging full thrust forward and for the life of me, I can hardly conceive of the force of will it must take to keep Connor's grasp firmly on the throttle. For a moment, fractal filaments of lightning as long as the Earth is wide make me think of the veins of an eye, one that is all pupil, no iris, and utterly uncaring of our plight even as we pierce the very centre of that staring eye, and I'm screaming once again.

The theoretical physicists say that information is one of the things the universe conserves, even in a black hole. They're not talking facts and figures, the capital of Nigeria, or the Best Film at the latest Oscars, they're talking about quantum mechanical waveforms that define even something as big as a person, as big as the *Naglfar*. (As big as a black hole...) It's impossible to know everything about ourselves, or anyone else, or any system equally as complex as we are. Which is why we rely on abstractions, why we're forced to make assumptions and sweeping generalisations.

None of that applies at some ineffable point in that incredible ride. Storm walls close around us, and we are buffeted, tossed like a cork in turbulent seas, knowing full well that this is a sheltered rock pool compared to the fearsome energies just beyond the heart of the malevolent vortex that would tear us and the *Naglfar* apart and care nothing for what it has so casually done. And as our destruction seems imminent, awareness *blooms*. Not like the unfurling of a delicate flower, but like the instant a nuclear bomb explodes, and even before a mushroom cloud can form, the information paradox resolves itself.

I can feel, can sense, every part of the *Naglfar* creak under the strain. And that should be terrifying of itself, but it isn't, somehow, despite the countless components on the cusp of critical failure. Because fail or not, it's all part of the same spaceship, the same whole, from the zero-g sanitation system to the infinite complexities of the fusion engines.

I know, for the first and only time in my life, everything that makes me *me*, everything that has led to this exact point in time and space. It's all laid out, in its tarnished glory, as systems crash and sparks fly, as alarms bleat impotently.

And I see, though see is utterly the wrong word, the same thing for Connor. See through his permanent state of tension, his all encompassing dislike and distrust of anyone and everyone. I understand *why* he neither likes nor loathes me any more than anyone else, the colour of my skin nothing more than an intellectual curiosity, something he could weaponise if he chose to. In that transcendent moment, I understand why he rarely does, even when pushed. More, I understand Connor himself, part and parcel, and not just in the now. I see the younger man he was when first we met, see the child that existed long before even that, and see the old, cantankerous man he will one day become.

The insight does nothing to sugar coat the pill. It renders him utterly, completely human. No cipher, no walls and barriers to hide behind, no pretence, no artifice, and most/worst of all, no projections of my own, false or otherwise. Unfiltered.

Even as the cosmos is turned inside out, I feel that intimate knowledge slipping away, and though it's like some previously unknown organ being painfully ripped out, it's probably for the best. At least as far as Connor and I are concerned. It would be excruciating to have such an intensely intimate relationship, one that even lovers can never hope to attain. But the memory--not of the *understanding*, but of the shared closeness--lingers, leaves behind traces written through and within me.

Here is a man I could and would spend the rest of my life with. Not because he's my perfect match, my one soul mate; I don't find him remotely attractive (not even--or especially--after a year cooped up together on the *Naglfar*), but because we have--in the maw of a black hole, in the information layer that surrounds a singularity--unveiled a fundamental connection, a pure form of love such as Christians speak of but (I suspect) rarely achieve. Like an elderly couple, long past the motions and expectations of romance, long past the need or desire to impress. Silent in our companionship, no need for words to describe or to explain or to excuse. No need even to be in the same room, the same city, the same country, to somehow *not* grow apart. It scares me more than perhaps it should that he must have experienced the same insights about me, scares me even deeper that he might *not* have done, that this is all one way. Scares me senseless that he wouldn't, couldn't, understand why it would be so unbearable to lose him from my life, even as I know (with absolute confidence) that such thoughts are from a former time, a former, lesser, me.

We are, and there is no better way to describe it even though it is still entirely inadequate, *entangled*.

What I cannot tell you about is the moment we emerge from the storm. A mote, ejected from the baleful eye of the black hole anomaly. There's a period of unknown, unfathomable duration when we are both insensible. Not unconscious; more as though we have been overloaded and are taking our time to reboot. Whatever was in the buffer is lost, and with it, the insight we have briefly gained. Though the memory of our insight persists, the moment of intimacy, and that is enough to rewrite everything we know. And, even if that is all that is left, it is still more than any two people on Earth have, now or perhaps ever.

Connor rubs the back of his neck, blinks owlishly at me as awareness returns. "Did we just...?"

"We survived," I say, cutting through any philosophical discussion. "But *where* are we?"

We're moving fast, that much is easy to tell; the debris that hangs around the black hole, impatiently waiting its turn to be shredded, looks like it is standing still. Even the star-field beyond is shifting. Behind us, the black hole is beginning to shrink, the vast turbulent surface curling itself into a sphere.

"The engines are still going?" he asks.

Miracle upon miracles. They are, though the port fusion reactor is red-lining and the only reason the alarm hasn't been noticed is because it has been competing with a dozen others, equally strident. I throttle it down a notch, and hope that will suffice, though suffice for what?

"Long range communications are shot." I remember the glowing array, the metal vaporising before our eyes. Not exactly repairable then, however good an engineer I claim to be.

"How about the short comms?"

"Still operational, far as I can tell." I shrug. We'd have to be lottery-winning lucky to get close enough for anyone to pick that up. Have to be heading almost directly towards the *Einstein*, going back the way we've come, an impossible U-turn, considering the shallow angle of our black hole dive.

Unless the rotation of a singularity...?

"What's that?" Connor interrupts.

Something fast, *awfully* fast, accelerating more than the pull of the black hole can explain. Something powered. That's why the *Naglfar*'s AI picks it out from the churning debris. Something artificial, heading our way. It will pass within a thousand klicks: in space terms, a peck on the cheek.

I zoom in on the speck, enlarge the image until we can see its elongated twin-engined Y shape.

It's the *Naglfar*.

Connor gapes. "That's... *impossible.* It must be another--"

"There *is* no other. It's us." I'm certain of it even as we speed towards our former selves.

Connor reaches for the comms. I grab and still his hand. "Two percent," I remind him.

He frowns though he realises and understands what I'm saying. The lingering connection means even if I didn't voice the words, didn't reach out my hand, he would (probably) understand. He lets his hand relax. The *Naglfar* speeding towards us is either us, circa half an hour or so ago, or some alternative reality version, seen through the twisted and warped fabric of space.

What could we say? To ourselves? That it is *safe*, and we'd made it through, despite the risks? Or that it is perilously, foolishly dangerous, and they shouldn't even attempt it?

What if it is only safe for this current version of us? What if receiving our warning is enough to upset the cosmic dice, to twist the odds out of their favour, to collapse the waveform into a different, mangled shape?

We have to let them make their own decisions. And, by the time those thoughts have fully formed, we're out of comms range anyway.

Above us, and hopefully waiting on this same trajectory, is the *Einstein*, and rescue, and the rest of our lives. And somewhere below and behind us now, an earlier, or alternative Connor, grips the ship's controls with whitened knuckles, stares deep into the heart of an impossible black hole storm, silently saying a prayer to evoke the gods of safe passage, as he bravely announces to his terrified partner:

"Here goes nothing!"

***Liam Hogan** is an award-winning short story writer, with stories in Best of British Science Fiction and in Best of British Fantasy (NewCon Press). He's been published by Analog, Daily Science Fiction, and Flame Tree Press, among others. He helps host live literary event Liars' League, volunteers at the creative writing charity Ministry of Stories, and lives and avoids work in London. More details at http://happyendingnotguaranteed.blogspot.co.uk*

The Art of War

Steve Burford

He was in his Studio the first time his world silently exploded.

As ever, he'd been completely absorbed, moving in and out of curator and subscriber P.O.V.s, trying to establish the best effect for a five minute loop of Angels circling the station, struggling to play up a sense of glory he didn't actually feel. He'd just plucked a squadron from the north of a moon's sky and reconfigured it in the east, where it could emerge, stirringly, if unrealistically, from over a low mountain range when the entire scene detonated in gouts of orange and red flame. His laboriously assembled collage disintegrated in burning pixels, and span into oblivion as multiple explosions ripped through it.

And then, it got stranger.

The dust and rock of the moon's surface blurred and reformed into the shattered roads and walkways of a city. Buildings he'd never seen before flowered, flared and fell back to their destruction. And among the buildings, glimpsed at their windows, behind the flames, people screamed without noise and died in the fire.

With a strangled gasp, Kelly lurched to his feet and punched the light panel by the side of his bunk. Fluorescents flickered on, superimposing the reality of his cramped billet over the horrific images being fed into his brain. Clawing at the Studio band, he tore it off from over his eyes, and flung it across the cubicle. The visions of destruction flared one last time in his visual cortex, and then were gone. It was only after he had recovered some control of his breathing that Kelly realised he had instinctively saved. Whatever that was that had just hit his Studio, it was now down in memory.

Half an hour later, he was hunched over a lukewarm coffee in the nearest mess hall, his hands still shaking as he clutched his mug.

"You look like shit." Jenkins sat down beside him.

"Thanks. So would you, if you'd just had your brains blown out of your head."

They might both have been reporters,

colleagues even, but Kelly would never have described Jenkins as a friend. Reporters, whatever their medium, were too cynical for easy friendships, and to cap that, Jenkins had never hidden his cynicism about Kelly's role as 'Official War Artist'. But, he was non-military, one of the precious few on the station, and that counted for something. Kelly took a deep breath, and told Jenkins what had happened to him.

"You should use words," Jenkins said. "They don't get to you the same way. Not after a while, anyway."

"Thanks for the tip." Kelly raised his coffee mug in an ironic gesture of gratitude.

"Seriously though. Could it have been some sort of feedback or overlay from something else on the Link?"

Kelly shook his head. "The Studio's a sealed unit. It has to be for copyright protection. I register and download finished works separately."

Jenkins shrugged. "Buggered if I know then. Maybe you should...."

"Join you?" The two men looked up. Kelly very deliberately thought of all of the station's military as 'grunts', irrespective of rank. It was one of a number of minor mental disciplines he used to keep that all-important distance between him and them. This grunt was called Barnes, and he was Jenkins's main source of station scuttlebutt. He sat, even though neither man had invited him to. He had a coffee with him, but put it down immediately and paid it no further attention. He leaned forward, voice low, constantly surveying the room as he spoke. "Heard the news?" It was his standard opening. "Prisoners. Six of them."

Kelly glanced at Jenkins but the reporter's eyes remained fixed on Barnes.

A war fought largely outside atmospheres rarely yielded up much in the way of P.O.W.s. Now, they had six. How that had happened, Barnes didn't know: something to do with a disabled shuttle and one hell of a lot of luck, he said. "Thanks," said Jenkins, once the soldier had told him all that he knew. He dug into an inner pocket and, without looking at it, slid a sachet across the table to the grunt. "Any more...."

"I'll be straight back to you." Barnes snatched up the sachet and was gone.

Kelly wondered briefly what Jenkins was paying his informants these days. Anything with more kick than the 'official' military issue had to be pretty nasty. "So what now?"

Jenkins sat, presumably thinking over what he'd just learned, then knocked back the last of his coffee and stood up. "I'm going to interview Commander Ferris." He laughed at the younger man's shocked surprise. "What? You want to know something, you go straight to the top. You? You go to bed." He tapped the side of his head. "And if anything else happens, you let me know, okay?"

Kelly followed Jenkins's advice but his dreams were filled with fire and destruction, and when he awoke he was soaked in sweat, his muscles sore as if he'd been running for his life.

He met the reporter again later that day in the same mess hall. "There are five of them," Jenkins said without preamble.

"So Barnes got it wrong." Kelly didn't bother to hide his contempt.

"No, Barnes got it right. There *were* six." Jenkins shrugged his shoulders.

"I want to see them." The words were out of Kelly's mouth before he'd thought them through. He saw something of his own surprise mirrored in Jenkins's face.

"Why?"

Kelly gave his best impression of one of Jenkins's shrugs. "It's my job."

"But...."

"Come on! When do I get to see anything more than grunts at their decks, or military flypasts? If that's all people want they can access library files. This is a chance to see something important. The other side. While we still have them."

"What? So, like, you're going to invite them to sit for a portrait? C'mon." Jenkins regarded the other man. Kelly sat, and waited. "All right!" Jenkins threw his hands up. "I'll see what I can fix."

"Thank you."

"Just one thing. A piece of advice." Jenkins checked around them before he spoke again. "On this station, it isn't 'The Other Side'. It's 'The Enemy'."

The message came though that night. The 'sitting' was on. Kelly gave the air one sharp punch of victory, and reached for his Studio deck and band to do the prelims for the next day. The Studio was up and running before he remembered why he hadn't accessed it since the last time - and by then it was too late.

Immediately, his 'vision' was filled by the noiseless inferno of the night before, but before he could shut it down, the red of conflagration morphed into the cold greys and black of ruins. Skeletons of buildings smouldered around him. Rubble covered the ground at his virtual feet. He caught a movement at the corner of his sight but couldn't rotate the P.O.V. Instead, he had to wait, with horrified fascination, for whatever it was to move around into his field of vision. It was the people he had glimpsed the night before, limping and shuffling through the remains of what must once have been their homes.

The ground lurched, and instinctively Kelly's arms flailed out. His annoyance at falling for an old V-Art trick quickly faded when he saw that it wasn't the 'ground' that had moved. Whoever was creating this scenario was moving the sun. It had been separately time-looped and was flying across the sky, dragging shadows across the devastation with an unnatural speed, and as they moved they uncovered horrors: torn, broken bodies. Like some grotesque *trompe l'oeuil,* the shifting light transformed the twisted forms of metal, glass and stone into corpses. Bodies, everywhere he looked, mutilated images of suffering and pain.

A figure separated itself from the moving shadows and stepped closer. It was carrying something. As it got closer, Kelly could see it was a child's body, lacerated almost beyond recognition. The walking figure raised the body as if in offering, and as it stepped closer still the shadows fell away from its face. The bearer was looking directly at Kelly.

Kelly screamed as he ripped off the band. If anyone heard, no-one came to investigate.

The next morning, Kelly's eyes were raw, and his head thick from lack sleep. When he arrived at the holding cell Jenkins's message had indicated, it was Barnes who was waiting outside. He pointed at Kelly's deck and band. "You can't take those in with you."

"What the fuck am I supposed to use then?"

Smirking, Barnes tossed him a pad of foolscap paper and a small bundle of pencils. "You can draw can't you?" His contempt was obvious. Kelly didn't care. It was mutual. It was all pointless military bullshit anyway. His retinal chips could store images for downloading later.

"You've got fifteen minutes," Barnes snapped. "Any trouble, shout and I'll be right in with my friend here." He patted the chargestick at his side. From his other side hung a gun.

"You're not coming in?" In spite of himself, Kelly was surprised and alarmed by that.

"Don't worry. There's only one in there." Barnes keyed the lock. "And like I said, you only have to squeal and I'll be in to break its fucking legs." The door opened. "Enjoy." Barnes held out his hand. Kelly stepped in. The door closed and sealed behind him.

The room was small and flooded with stark, white light. Two black chairs were fused to the floor facing each other. In one of them sat the Alend.

It was staring at the floor, and did not look up. It was humanoid. From a distance, it could even have been human. A little taller than average perhaps, and paler. Its skin had a blueish tinge but that could have been the reflected hues of the military fatigues it had been dressed in.

Kelly crossed the cell to sit down facing it. He wondered if the alien knew what it was there for. Briefly he considered saying something, maybe pantomiming an explanation, but faced with an unresponsive creature that, as far as they knew, spoke no human language, and couldn't be expected to recognise human gestures, he abandoned the idea. He licked his lips and gathered his distracted thoughts. He flipped over the pad's cover, took out one of the pencils, and very deliberately started work at this grim mockery of a sitting.

Years of drawing human subjects had conditioned Kelly's hand to produce lines and planes which he now found simply weren't there in the Alend. Textures melted into surprising smoothness, musculature shifted subtly, unexpectedly. There were a thousand differences between this and a human, each of them almost imperceptible on their own, but together creating a totality that was ... alien. It took Kelly over four attempts, four pages of angrily crossed out work, before he finally fell into the rhythm of his art, eyes moving smoothly up and down between alien and image on paper, the two becoming one for him. As ever, when he was in this frame of mind he lost track of time. So he had no idea how long it was before the alien finally looked up and for the first time he saw its eyes.

They were the eyes he had seen in his Studio the night before. They were the eyes of the man who had held out to him the body of the child like a sacrifice. At the instant of eye-contact, Kelly was back in the smoking city, surrounded by the misery, and this time he swore he could hear the moans and the crying, smell the smoke and the blood.

The vision was momentary, and broken by a sudden, sharp tugging sensation. With dizzying speed, Kelly was brought back to reality in time to see the Alend seating itself once more in front of him. It had been out of its chair! Had it attacked? Was he injured? Bleeding? A frantic scan revealed no wound. Then what...? The Alend was sitting, facing him, as unreadable as before, but now, in its hands were two sheets of paper. It had torn them from Kelly's pad and snatched the pencil he had been using. As Kelly watched, the prisoner unfastened its fatigues, pushed in the paper and pencil, refastened the cloth then smoothed it down with one hand.

Kelly jumped at the sudden hiss of the cell door's unsealing. "All right Picasso. Time's up." Unsteadily, Kelly rose to face Barnes. Should he say anything? He could easily guess how the grunt would react to his having let a prisoner take anything off him, even if it was only paper and a pencil.

He went to speak. Barnes smirked. "Get its good side?"

Kelly shut his mouth, and exited the cell. "I'll be back the same time tomorrow," he said over his shoulder.

It was another two days before Kelly saw Jenkins again, and when he finally opened his door to the reporter's insistent knocking, there was no missing the shock on Jenkins's face at his altered appearance. "You look like..," Jenkins began.

"I know. Get in." As Jenkins entered, Kelly looked past him up and down the corridor. All clear. He closed the door.

"So what's...." Before Jenkins could say any more, Kelly shoved a tube of rolled-up paper into his hands. Jenkins raised his eyebrows but unrolled the papers without further words, quickly scanned the drawings on them, rolled them up again and handed them back. "So?" he said.

"They're not mine." It was an effort for Kelly to keep his voice steady. "They're the Alend's."

"What? How?"

"I gave it... I gave *him* paper and pencils."

"And Barnes let you?"

"He didn't see. How did you know it was Barnes?"

"He told me. During one of our 'transactions.'"

"Right. He tell you anything else?"

Jenkins looked away. "He said there are only three Alends now."

Kelly collapsed onto his bunk. "Three! "That means three dead. Three dead and three times...." He looked up at Jenkins. "I knew it. On some level, I knew it." He reached for his Studio deck. "Those drawings are amazing," he said as he stabbed at his deck, "but this is what's really important. This is what you've got to see." Deck prepped, he thrust the band at Jenkins. Reluctantly, the other man took it, hesitated, then wrapped it over his eyes.

Five minutes later, he too sank down onto the edge of Kelly's bunk. "Christ!" he whispered. "I didn't know." His skin looked grey.

Kelly took the band back. "You look like shit."

"I can't ... I can't get my thoughts...." Jenkins shook his head like a dreamer struggling to wake. "I can't fucking concentrate!"

"It's the images. They're very powerful."

"So many.... Where the hell did they come from?"

"The Alends. And don't ask me how. I don't know. I only know this has come from them. And the Alend in the cell? He's in the Studio images." Kelly took a deep breath. "So far, I've had three ... experiences in my Studio, three separate packages of information. Three, Jenkins. Don't you see?" Kelly leaned in close to the reporter. "It's killing them to get this to us." He laughed, an ugly, fractured sound. "Talk about dying for your art."

"You don't know...." Jenkins broke off, flinging his arms up in front of his face as if to ward off some sudden blow. When nothing happened he lowered them shakily, breathing hard, his face glistening with sweat. "I thought...."

"It's all right. I get that too. Sudden flashes like intense memories. I think it's the brain's way of trying to process the images fired into it. Don't worry. Most of it happens when you're asleep. Yeah, your dreams will be pretty intense for a while."

"Bastard!"

There was a strained silence as the two of them sat on the bunk, neither looking at the other. It was Jenkins who finally spoke first. "All right. So, you've got this stuff." He gestured towards the deck and the papers. "What are you going to do with it?"

Kelly's voice was almost level. "What I always do. Upload it to the Link."

"What! If you think you can get away with that then this stuff really has melted your brain! The military would never pass it. It's pure Alend propaganda."

"It's another side to the story."

"Same thing!"

Kelly jumped up from the bunk and began pacing the small room. "I didn't expect this from you, Jenkins. I mean, look at us. What do we ever really achieve around here? They let us see grunts on parade. I send pictures and you send words back home so people can feel proud, while in reality, people are dying, them *and* us. No-one back home knows what's really going on, and now I've got a chance to show them at least part of it."

"Maybe they don't want to know what's *really* going on," Jenkins said in a low voice.

"Maybe they need to. Maybe too many people with too much power are making too much money out of this war. Have you ever considered that?"

"Of course I have. I've been dealing with this shit since before you stuck your first band on your head."

Kelly leant over him, hands curled into fists. "Then perhaps you've been dealing with it too long! Perhaps you didn't see when you stopped being a reporter and became just another Link entertainer."

"I know what I am." Jenkins's words were quiet, but his eyes narrowed.

There was another brittle silence.

"The whole thing's academic anyway," Jenkins said. "There's no way the military would pass it."

"Who says they're ever going to see it? Do they ever see those little sachets you bring with you to throw around the mess halls? I'll find a way." Jenkins lurched to his feet. "Wait." Kelly paused as if uncertain how to go on. When he spoke again his voice was lower and softer, heavy with emotion of a different kind. "There is another reason I'm doing this. Not just because I think it's part of a wider truth, not just because people are dying to get this to me. It's ... it's because what they're giving me is so much_*better* than anything I've ever done, better than anything I could *ever* do. I've been an artist all my life. It's all I've ever wanted to do. But I have never made anything that speaks to me the way this Alend work does. It's real. It's raw. It's... *true.* I can't turn my back on that, I just can't." He held his hands out in appeal. "Can you understand that?"

Jenkins stood, regarding the other man. "No." He turned his back on Kelly and opened the door. In the corridor outside he stopped. He spoke without looking back, his voice monotonous. "I nearly forgot. I had to tell you that the Alends, the ones we still have, are going. They're being shipped to Earth in the next couple of days. You'll get one more sitting." He left.

Kelly sat in his room and waited for the footsteps, the knock on the door, and the grunts dragging him off to court-martial or a beating or whatever it was they would do to him once Jenkins told them what he was planning. But the soldiers didn't come, and Kelly fell asleep and dreamed of the Alend homeworld burning while no-one on Earth knew.

Barnes was outside the cell again the next day, with the same scornful expression. Kelly ignored him. If this was to be his last session then he had something very important to do.

As before, the alien was sitting waiting for him. Kelly had spent hours puzzling over the problem of communication, when the answer had been in front of them all along. Kelly sat down and flipped back the top page of his pad. "I hope you get this," he said, more for himself than for the prisoner, and he showed the Alend the picture he had drawn. It was a simple sketch, crude even. To the right were the Studio images, the buildings, the dying Alends. To the left was a representation of Kelly himself surrounded by humans. Kelly was standing with his arm outstretched towards the alien devastation, showing humanity the results of its war efforts.

The alien sat and looked at the work. Its face did not change. After five minutes Kelly sighed, closed the pad and turned back towards the door. He hoped the message had got through. He hoped the Alend understood now that its comrades had not died in vain.

He had only about a second to register the pressure of a hand on his shoulder before he was yanked backwards and fell to the floor, papers from the pad flying chaotically around him. The Alend was on top of him, crushing the breath out of him, twisting his arm hard behind his back. "No! Wait! I...." Something sharp was jammed into the fleshy part of his throat. Kelly bit back his cries. The Alend looked down at him, its face as impassive as ever. Its breathing was even, as if this exertion had cost no effort at all, but its breath was unnaturally hot on Kelly's cheek.

With a twist of his arm, the alien manoeuvred Kelly upright again. He felt the sting of whatever it was at his throat, and the slow, warm trickle of blood down his skin. The Alend pushed him towards the door, stopped, twisted and jabbed again. Kelly understood. "Open up!" he called.

"Quick today weren't you?" Barnes mocked, as the door unsealed. "What's up? You...?" He tailed off as he took in the situation. Kelly saw his hand jerk towards the holstered chargestick. The Alend wrenched at Kelly's arm, and the artist cried out in pain. Barnes reluctantly raised his hands. Slowly, the Alend pushed its human hostage through the door of the cell, never taking its eyes from Barnes who backed away before it. Kelly was babbling now through his fear and pain, the words "No, Please, no!" spilling from his mouth. He was past knowing whether they were for Barnes, the alien or both.

Outside the cell, the alien gestured for Barnes to lie face down on the floor. The soldier hesitated. The Alend pushed Kelly's arm higher up his back. Kelly shrieked. "All right! All right!" Slowly, Barnes lay on the floor, the side with his gun holster facing the alien. The Alend released Kelly's arm, still using its other hand to hold its weapon at the artist's throat. A kick to the back of his legs sent Kelly kneeling to the ground. Reaching down, the alien yanked Barnes's gun from its holster, and gave Kelly a savage push, so that the artist collapsed sobbing in a heap on the soldier. Looking up, Kelly saw the unreadable alien face behind the barrel of the gun as it straightened and took aim at both him and the soldier. He screamed.

With a dull thud, the Alend's head exploded, showering Kelly with alien blood and bone. Its body flew forwards, landing at his side, its eyes open and staring at the artist. They were the eyes he had seen in his Studio. One of the Alend's arms was flung out as if accusing the human. In its hand, the pencil Kelly had given it, whittled to a sharp point. Kelly could still see his own blood on it. It was the last thing he saw before someone shot him full of meds and he was dragged away.

"He'll be all right?"

"I suppose so. He's still with the medics."

"He could have died."

"Unlikely. There was an armed squad literally round the corner."

Jenkins leaned forward in his chair to face Station Commander Ferris across her desk. "So what now? You've taken his deck?"

"Of course. And the doctor's removing his retinal chips as we speak. Ops are very excited. They believe that if we retro-engineer the viruses and subliminals embedded in the images the Alends were firing into Kelly's brain, we could learn more about the Enemy in one go than we have throughout the whole of this war so far." The Commander gave a small smile. "That's what made the images so compelling you see. Neural warfare."

"Is that all?" Even now, Jenkins had to consciously fight down the flood of memories that threatened to rise in his head at the mere mention of what he had seen, and Commander Ferris had not.

"Of course. What else could t have been? And just think," she added, "what that could have done had it been uploaded to the Link."

"We set him up didn't we?" Jenkins said quietly. "We pushed Kelly in with the Alend and sat back to see what would happen."

Ferris shook her head. "Kelly did just what he wanted to do. We didn't order, we didn't even suggest. And we did make sure he wasn't too badly hurt. But, it was something we had to do. It was obvious the Alend were up to something. Six of them all at once? It was far too good to be true. Our Mr. Kelly was very helpful and he has done humanity a great service."

"But how did they do it, access his Studio I mean, and why him in the first place?"

Ferris steepled her fingers. "That we don't know yet. There are some pretty fancy theories flying around but most of them agree that it just came down to proximity. So you can be damn sure we won't be taking any more prisoners any time soon. It could have had something to do with the Studio facility Kelly used as well, I suppose, or it could have been something actually in Kelly's brain. That's another thing the doctors are looking into." Jenkins glanced up sharply at that, but Ferris paid no heed and carried on. "He could simply have been too willing to believe. Artists are so… receptive, aren't they?"

"Then why did the Alend attack him then in the end?"

Ferris gave a low, mirthless laugh. "Again, any number of suggestions. We made sure it knew it was being shipped to Earth. It could have thought the game was up and decided to make a last ditch bid for freedom." She leant back in her chair. "I do have my own pet theory though. I think it may have been because of that picture Kelly showed it. He meant it as a promise of what he was going to do. I think the Alend took it as a statement of what Kelly had actually done, so proving that he'd outlived his usefulness. They're a very literal-minded race, you know. You can see it clearly in their battle strategy. A pity Kelly never asked us about that." She sighed exaggeratedly. "Art can be so hard to interpret, can't it?"

Jenkins stood, his face tight.

"Before you leave." Ferris opened a drawer in her desk and took out a small pile of plastic sachets. "I thought you'd probably used up most of your stock over recent days." She placed a slightly larger, pale blue sachet on top of the others. "And something extra for you, of course."

Jenkins stared at the pile for long seconds then, with a convulsive movement, snatched the sachets up and shoved them into his jacket pockets. "And well done," Ferris concluded. "Another mission carried out successfully."

"Mission?" Jenkins winced as if she had struck him. "Nothing so grand, Commander. Just one more bit of treachery for the cause."

Ferris tutted. "As ever, Mr. Jenkins, you underestimate yourself." She sat back in her chair and regarded him thoughtfully, a small smile on her thin lips. "No, I truly think it could be said that in your own way you could be described as something of an artist."

***Steve Burford** has been writing for a number of years now in a variety of genres for a range of publications. His most successful work has probably been a series of police procedural novels, but his first love remains SF.*

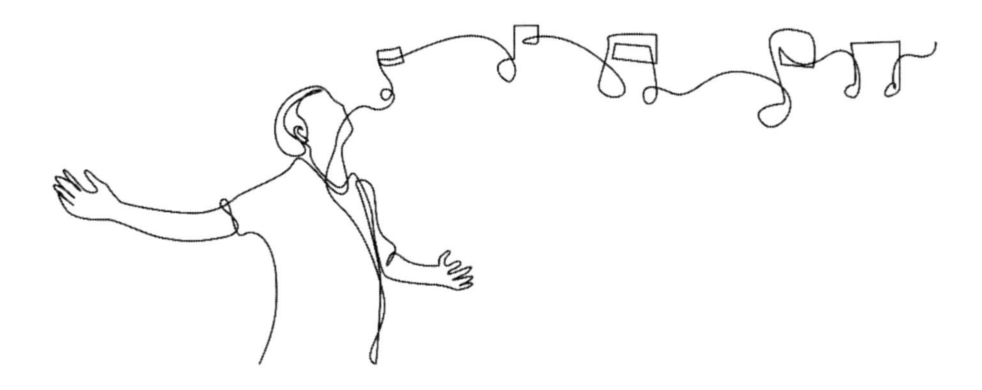

Song of Unmaking

Jacey Bedford

Peter inhaled the last swirl of the sickly-sweet vapour as he reached to snuff out the burner. The dry saucer was sugared with the deposits from dozens of candle-powered dreams. His mind drifted elsewhere and his reactions were slow. Tomorrow would add burnt fingers to his catalogue of misery, but tonight would be... ah! It would be magic.

He settled back against the pillows on top of the bedcover, checking with the ponderous care of the drunkard that he had stoppered the tiny bottle of Oblivion properly. Last week he'd left it loose and the inoffensive-looking oil had evaporated before he'd discovered his mistake. Once, not so long ago, in another life and with another name, he'd used it whenever he felt the need. Memory kindly glossed over the fact that he'd hardly ever bothered with the stuff.

The Oblivion was taking over now, drawing him out of his body, spinning his senses, teasing the frayed ends of his nerves into a silken gossamer thread, a frail anchor to reality. It held him suspended in a hypnotic trance and he hovered, waiting for it to fall away and release him to his dream-world paradise.

It didn't.

Instead, he tasted peaches on the back of his tongue Damn! What a waste. There was always a chance—it said so in the small print—that Oblivion would do the opposite of what its advertising campaign promised. Instead of escaping to a fantasy, he was going to revisit his past. Fuck! He was already sliding under.

He focused on the mirror, saw himself, sprawled against the gaudy coverlet, his eyes glazed and his mouth slack. He was surrounded by the everyday clutter of Julie's cheap apartment, and though he'd been here for four months he still looked out of place.

Given time he would become as pale and pinched as Julie and the kids. He saw the recent lines around his mouth turning down at the edges. Stress? Strain? Worry? All three in equal measure, he decided, seasoned with a generous portion of self-contempt!

"It's not my fault!" He protested, but the judge and jury in the Oblivion bottle tried him in his absence and found him guilty.

He had been the man with everything. The cliché character of the poor kid who struck it rich by virtue of his talent, good looks and on-stage charisma. He'd become Hero Young (his manager chose the name) and had never looked back. He'd married his manager's daughter—it seemed like a wise move when, pregnant with his second child, she had taken over from her dad and given him an ultimatum. From that moment on she ran him like the big business he had become. Prestige concerts in New York, followed by Rome, Moscow and Tokyo; a series of recordings which had topped the US charts on the day of release.

Even the President was a fan.

That had been the start of the nightmare. He could only assume that the DHS, CIA, FBI or some other less obvious, but equally powerful, department, known only by its initials, had run a routine investigation before they'd allow his vocal chords into the White House. Instead of an invitation to sing, he was summoned to a small building outside the city limits, behind the White Flint Mall off Rockville Pike. It looked innocuous enough, and so did the people who met him there.

It was only later that he came to understand that their powers were not limited by conventions. If they wanted him, even his star status provided minimal protection. He was incredulous at first. The whole thing was so far-fetched that if it had been written up in the National Enquirer it would have looked like no more than silly-season speculation.

Who would possibly believe that there were singers who had such power and resonance that by their voice alone they could destroy? Unmake. Their voices acted as the focus some kind of kinetic power which could be harnessed to rearrange basic molecular structure. It was kids' comic book stuff, but Hero had not laughed.

The Oblivion-induced dream leaped through that unsettling period of invitation, persuasion, and, finally, coercion. He relived a super-smooth ride in a limo. There was a brief flash of silver from the Potomac as they headed out across the bridge on a long ride to God knows where, then the arrival, the briefing and suddenly he was standing in a studio, a huge barn of a place. It was an impossible size for recording, and besides, there were no microphones anyway. Three white-coated boffins stood behind an armoured glass observation window, one with a tablet and pen. The pair of Bureau minders who had made sure he was on time for this appointment stood behind them, stiff and watchful.

A panel in the far wall slid back with a low rumble to reveal a circular tower fully five metres high, built of old-fashioned bricks and mortar.

"Right, Mr. Young. That's your target Remember all that you've been told and use whatever technique you find most natural." The disembodied voice came over the speaker system, and behind the window he could see the boffins watching ready to measure, calculate and evaluate.

Explanations had been brief, instructions practically non-existent, this was a test of his potential—of the instinctive use of whatever kinetic power he might have. He was afraid, but he was also intensely curious. The possibilities were petrifying, but at the same time exhilarating.

His sensible-self, with all the benefit of hindsight, screamed at his dream-self to fake it. Don't let them see. Don't let them measure. Leave the monster sleeping inside.

But his dream-self resolutely stuck to the script.

He began, low and resonant, a familiar tune, but lonely without instrumentation. He was nervous as he never was on stage and it affected his breathing and his voice control. He felt the faint tremor in the notes and stopped.

"Rerun. All right, Mr. Young, in your own time." The disembodied voice wasn't going to let him get away with it.

All right—get the nerves under control. It's like an audition. If he did it right they would give him—what? A job?

He shrugged his shoulders a few times to remove any lingering stiffness and yawned, letting the yawn extend into a low, resonant note with his throat open and relaxed. That was better. He ahhed softly up and down a scale, not trying to push any power out. His throat relaxed and he regained confidence.

Use a familiar song, they had said. He had chosen "Homeland", or it had chosen him? The song was an anthem for the world's displaced people, starting gently and building to musical climax, the intensity nothing to do with volume and everything to do with passion. Reaching the third verse, he mentally shifted up a gear until the resonance was part of his whole body. It vibrated upwards from the soles of his feet to the tips of his fingers. His skull was a drum skin, throbbing with the rhythm. The sound rose in a soaring crescendo. He was giving it all he'd got. It was as far as he could go—but that part of him which always stood apart from the song said it wasn't enough!

His eyes flickered to the boffins, encased in the safety of their soundproof room with their various 'ometers, and at that moment he hated them for bringing him here and making him go through all this only to discover that he wasn't what they suspected him to be. Resentment bubbled up along with disappointment and bitterness, hate and fear.

Something connected in his brain. Maybe he hadn't reached his limit. The notes soared and he broke through into a new world of sound that was beyond ears.

The whole building shook, and the tower began to rock and crumble. The bricks dissolved into nothing. He'd reached his limit and passed it. Hypnotised by the chaos, he couldn't stop now.

What singer can resist knowing what his audience thinks? Still singing, he turned to glance at the boffins to catch their reaction. Briefly he saw the fear on their faces and realised he was aiming the destructive force straight at them. He snapped his jaws shut on the song, but it was too late. It played out in slow-mo. One white-coated figure leapt towards the glass barrier shouting something and waving wildly while the others ducked away. The armoured glass screen shattered explosively and the man behind it collided with the shock wave and the shards, In one horrific instant he ceased to be.

Hero's throat constricted. The remains of the tower stabilised. He stood stunned, staring in horror at the wreckage. He tasted the dust of destruction floating in the still air and his legs began to fold under him. He would have fallen except for his two minders who emerged at a run and steadied him, or was their firm grasp more of a restraint?

"Oh my God!" The boffins emerged slowly and cautiously from the remains of their ruined control booth, white faced beneath the dust from the debris. "Weaver's gone! Just gone...."

They looked at Hero, their faces masks of shock. He didn't mean to.... He didn't mean to! They must believe that. Oh, God, a man had died.

"Take him to the hospitality suite." A new voice, calm and confident, cut through the chaos and a uniformed figure emerged from the observation gallery. "Give Mr. Young whatever he wants, but for now he should remain with us. There will be more tests to run, this degree of talent is remarkable without training."

Hadn't they seen enough? It was too dangerous. He had unmade a man! Hero knew that whatever their threats he'd finished with the whole business. But they had him as their—what? Guest? Test subject? Prisoner? The minders led him away and he followed them meekly while his mind raced.

"Steady, now, Mr. Young." One of his minders said. "The first time's always the worst. You'll find it much easier next time."

Next time! They wanted him to do it again. They were mad—or he was!

He smiled vacantly, but it was only a mask to hide his inner confusion. If he could do this thing—if by singing he could unmake solid bricks and human flesh—how would he ever dare to appear on stage again? There would be no next time. Hero Young had given his last performance.

Getting away was the problem. Sessions of instruction followed, then more tests, but despite their best efforts, they couldn't induce him to show even the slightest kinetic ability. One boffin said he'd burned out, another suspected him of faking, but they couldn't prove it either way and finally, with much reluctance and signing of secrecy documents, they had to let him go. His silence was assured by the threat of a murder charge hanging over his head should he step out of line.

He wondered whether they would have let him walk if he had been a nobody. Would he have met with some kind of accident? Hero Young was not so easy to dispose of. He had friends, well connected to the media, who knew his last known appointment had been with the President's security people.

But given enough time, they could rearrange his life. He was out, for now, but was he free? Had they really let him go?

He doubted it.

So he quit! Walked out on his contracts. Left home. Left Maura, wife, manager, mother of his children, to sort out the mess and pay off the promoters. He and Maura were more of a business partnership than a marriage these days, but, God, it had taken all his strength to leave Sara and little Jessie. Only the thought of hurting them accidentally had stiffened his resolve.

His money bought him a fast and unorthodox route out of the country and a new identity, but even after two years he still looked over his shoulder. He ended up in England where, despite his popularity in the USA, Canada and the Far East, he had never quite made it. It had been his one remaining ambition to crack the British music scene, but now he was thankful for the anonymity.

The Oblivion began to wear off, letting his mind merge back into his body. He gradually became aware of his surroundings. Ruby was watching from the doorway, her eyes too knowing for her twelve-year-old face. Julie's kids had to grow up fast. How long had she been there? Sometimes he caught her watching him as if she still couldn't quite believe who he was.

"When you're asleep you look just like him."

"Yeah, I'm Hero Young, and Elvis works in the local diner. You'd do better to throw out those old posters. There are plenty of better singers around."

"No one like him. You look so much like him I wish you could sing like him too.

"If I could I wouldn't be sitting here in Leeds with no cash in my pocket? I told you I'm tone deaf. Can't sing a note."

"You couldn't play keyboards like you do if you were tone deaf."

"It's only like pushing buttons on a machine. My fingers work, it's my voice that doesn't!"

He never knew whether Ruby really believed that tale or whether she played along to humour him. It was just his luck to find that Julie's daughter was one of the few British fans of the late Hero Young. Punters in the music business were fickle. Most of his fans had moved on to new idols after news of Hero's death in the proverbial rock-star private plane crash.

Grimly he wondered whether it was Maura's work or whether the Bureau had a hand in the cover up of his disappearance. It would be too convenient for them if they ever caught up with him. There would be no civil rights for a dead man.

Was the Bureau fully operational in England? He didn't doubt that they had some influence over here, but he hoped that they were less omnipotent than back home. There had been a time when the British Prime Minister had played along with America, but thankfully the Saudi debacle had ended all that.

"Wayne's been crying," Ruby said.

Peter's brain cleared quickly and he went to check on the younger children. He didn't need to, Ruby had been the babysitter of the family since the age of seven, but he felt that since he was there he should do something to help. He did a quick head count in the boys' room. Wayne and Darren were at opposite ends of a narrow bed and Dean, a mischievous toddler, was safely behind bars in an old-fashioned cot, tangled up in a crumpled quilt with his feet up on the pillow.

Julie was on late shift again behind the bar in the too-chic-for-its-own-good club where Peter had played the grand piano until he had been fired for refusing to play a tune for one of the customers. The lady had asked for 'Homeland'.

It was the song with which he had unmade the boffin.

The door clicked softly in the night-time silence and a sleepy child's voice called out,

"Is that you, Mummy?"

"Shh! Yes. Don't wake Dean, Lovey." Julie leaned against the door jamb to take her shoes off and flex her aching feet against the cold, tiled floor.

"I want a wee."

"Come on then. Quietly. Slip your shoes on."

"Do I have to?"

"Yes, your feet will get cold."

Wayne heaved himself out of the tumble of bedclothes and staggered sleepily to the bathroom, unfastened shoes flapping. He lifted the lavatory seat and peed over the edge of the pot, splashing the wall-covering which already curled at the edges in protest at being in close proximity to three small boys with erratic toilet habits.

Julie stood over him then absentmindedly grabbed a handful of paper, wiping off the worst of the wetness as her four-year-old crumpled back into bed, asleep before he even pulled the covers back over himself. She eased off his shoes and dropped them on the floor alongside his dirty clothes, rolled him into the middle of the mattress and flopped the quilt on to his thin body.

She tiptoed through the living room to avoid waking Ruby who had slept on the sofa since Peter moved in. She knew Peter felt guilty about ousting the child from the bed she had shared with her mother, but Ruby was adaptable—she'd spent half her life on that sofa.

Julie tiptoed in to the bedroom, closed the door against the sleeping children and risked the dim glow from a bedside lamp. Her feet ached from the stiletto heels and pointy toes of the sixties-style shoes which were part of her uniform. She slipped out of the white leatherette miniskirt, pulled off the black and white sleeveless polo neck top with the keyhole that showed her cleavage to best advantage and dropped both in turn on to a chair. Her spine felt as though it had knots in it. She looked over at Peter, fast asleep with one naked leg half on top of the quilt revealing his strong back and a strip of smooth golden flesh down his hip to his leg. She'd never had a man like this before. His body would have impressed her even if she hadn't recognised him from all of Ruby's press cuttings. His hair had fooled her at first. Hero Young had been blessed with long harvest-blond hair and Peter's hair was a close-cut mousy brown, his natural colour probably.

She didn't know why he was on the run and she didn't want to know. Everyone was on the run from something. She was grateful that she had him. To everyone else he was Peter Beck, unemployed piano player, but to Julie he was Hero Young, megastar.

Of course, Julie was careful not to ask about his past. There was always the thought in the back of her mind that she might be wrong, that he might be plain Peter Beck after all, and she would make an idiot of herself. She preferred to keep her dreams.

She stretched her aching shoulders and looked again at her lover as she reached to turn out the lamp. He stirred as she slipped her cold, thin body next to his. Oh well, perhaps she wasn't that tired!

Ruby's early morning call was right on time. Dean's usual ritual began at 6.30 when he awoke with the first sound of footsteps in the apartment upstairs.

"Uby! Uby!"

Ruby cursed. He didn't even bother to shout for Mum now; she was always dead to the world at this hour, and even the baby of the family was wary of his mother's early morning temper.

"Uby!"

She scowled at him as she rammed a hastily made jam sandwich through the cage bars of his cot.

"Deanie Boy want drinkies?" Ruby asked.

The infant gurgled contentedly around the masticated crusts.

"Say 'drinkie', Dean. Say 'drinkie' for Uby." Ruby dangled the feeder cup tantalisingly out of reach.

"Din."

"Oh well, have it your own way then." Ruby got fed up and thrust the cup through the bars spraying droplets of deep red fruit juice from the holes in the spout in a perfect arc over the sheet

She left him to settle down with his breakfast and returned to her makeshift bed in the living room. She hated it. She used to lie there wishing that her latest uncle would get bored so that she could regain her place next to Mum. Now, at twelve, she was nearly grown. Ruby still wanted her half of the bed, but in her dreams it was her mother who slept on the sofa.

Ruby wasn't tired enough to nod off again, so she pulled on the same undies and dress that she had worn yesterday and let herself out of the front door.

She went along the corridor and out on to the balcony which overlooked the quadrangle, the planners' posh name for the depressing square of artificial turf which provided the only hint of colour between the four tall, grey blocks that made up The Square. Later in the day the kids would gather here, but now it was empty—littered only with scrunched up cans from the previous night's occupancy. Good! that meant that the rubbish carts hadn't been yet so there was still time to intercept Maggie on her way home from work.

Maggie had been Ruby's favourite person since she discovered that the plump black woman worked in the all-night cafe at the bottom of the Headrow. She arrived home as the world was waking and if she managed to hitch her usual ride with Eddie on the rubbish cart, her goody bag would still be warm.

There was never any guessing what Maggie's leftover treat would be, but Ruby prayed for waffles, hot and sticky with syrup. Her mouth began to water in anticipation as she skipped across the balcony and down the steps to wait in the tunnel which led to the outside world.

The low rumbling vibration of the solectric motor soothed the burning ache in Maggie's feet as she leaned back in the spare seat in the cab. She and Eddie sat in companionable silence. He was an easy friend to have, so they didn't need to fill in the empty spaces between bouts of conversation.

As the cart pulled into the service bay, a figure emerged from the shadows of the tunnel. Eddie waved a hand towards the windscreen.

"It's the kid again. Don't you ever get sick of her hanging about?"

"Yeah. Sometimes, but she needs a place to hide and someone outside her family to talk to, and I'm it. I only get her company so early on account of this." Maggie waved the food bag. "Pizza this morning. Not madam's favourite, or mine either, but it's free and it fills the hole where breakfast should be. Times are too hard to let it waste."

"Eric's pay rise never came through then?"

"When they'd finished their reports he was damn lucky to keep his job; no chance of a raise, now or ever! There'd be a hundred people willing to take his place on half pay! And we heard yesterday that the rent on this place is going up again at the end of the month."

"It's a shame you lost your other job, the one that if you told me about it, you'd have to shoot me. They must have paid well."

"Yeah!" Maggie didn't want to discuss what was still a sore point. She had known Eddie for almost thirty years, but they'd lost touch when Maggie had accepted a place in the new government programme.

Then three years ago it had all fallen apart and she came home with her husband, a minor civil servant. She knew Eddie was curious about what she'd been doing and what had gone wrong, but Maggie couldn't tell him. If she didn't shoot him, someone else would.

As the refuse cart rattled off into the morning Ruby detached herself from the shadow of the wall and smiled a bright brittle smile for Maggie's benefit and called out, "You're early! Eddie must be on the morning run again."

"It saves my aching feet when he is." Maggie's smile was tired

Ruby's eyes strayed past the round black face to the carry-home bag.

"Pizza," Maggie said.

"Oh."

"You don't have to eat it."

"Oh no. I didn't mean... That is, yes. I'd like some, please."

"OK. You take my key and run on ahead. I want the table set by the time I get there. Do it quietly, don't wake Eric."

Ruby never needed inviting twice. The child took the proffered key and scampered up the four flights of stairs while Maggie toiled slowly up behind her, cursing the broken lift.

They ate lukewarm, leathery pizza in silence. Ruby tried not to look at the portion put by for Maggie's stringy, white husband. She knew better than to ask for more. Like most adults Maggie was always short-tempered when she was tired and so Ruby had learned to eat and run.

"I'll wash up," she offered. "You go to bed. I'll drop the latch when I leave."

Maggie nodded and disappeared in the direction of the bedroom while Ruby nuked a jug of water for the washing up. Maggie never used the built-in dishwasher or the water heating system on account of the high fuel bills.

Ruby cut a small sliver from the remaining slice of Pizza. Eric would never know. He would get up for work as Maggie fell asleep and breakfast would be a memory by the time they saw each other again. Licking her fingers Ruby let herself out and ran back home to see what mischief the boys had managed while her back was turned.

Eric lay sprawled across the middle of the bed and Maggie had to gently nudge him to one side so she could slide in beside him, her ample black next to his bony white.

He half-opened his eyes, smiled sleepily and whispered, "Hey."

"Hey." She waited for him to roll over then she snuggled up to him, feeling his arms around her middle. They had maybe half an hour before he had to get up for work, so better make the most of it.

The alarm clock shattered Maggie's cosy moment and she felt Eric stir and lift his head from where it rested between her breasts. He rolled over with a groan and tried to sit up on the edge of the bed, but Maggie held on to his arm for a moment before relinquishing him to the world and his day job.

"What's for breakfast?" he asked.

"Pizza."

"Ugh!" He pulled on his trousers and socks and stood up.

"Better than nothing."

" I suppose.

"There's plenty left."

"No Ruby this morning, then, if there's plenty left?" He found the shirt Maggie had laid out for him.

"Yeah, she was here."

"I don't think she should hang around so much. She should look to her own family first. What are her parents thinking of, letting her out at all hours of the day and night?"

"There is no dad, though her mum's never short of company. The kid's a bit sly at times, maybe, but underneath all that streetwise act she's only a kid. She's probably glad to get away from those baby brothers of hers."

"Well, I still don't like it. We've got troubles enough of our own. Without that pay rise I don't know how we'll manage. Maybe I could get some sort of moonlighting, job but I'm too old for labouring and there's not much call for part-time clerks."

His droopy shoulders drooped still further.

She put out a hand and let it rest lightly on his arm. "I love you."

"You could have done better than me, Mags. Personnel could have fixed you up with..."

"Hush-up. Did I ever say I wanted anyone else?"

"Don't pretend that if you'd had a free choice you'd have picked me."

"No, I wouldn't—and that would have been the biggest mistake of my life. I'm just sorry you got booted out when I did... Without me you might still have had your old job. Maybe you'd have been department head by now."

He put his hand over hers. "I'd rather have you and my crummy clerk's job. It wasn't right that they closed down the programme, Mags. You didn't deserve that, neither losing the job nor having the surgery."

Maggie put her hand to her throat. There was no visible scar, but the damage had been done. She'd lost her singing voice. Damn near lost her speaking voice too. It still sounded funny--like there was a band squeezing her throat closed.

"You know, I don't mind not being able to shatter concrete with my voice, but I sure miss being able to sing. Just ordinary singing. They took that away from me as well."

Eric said nothing, just held on to Maggie's hand.

She sighed. She knew why they'd done it. They daren't release fully functioning kinetic singers from a project so secret that not even the highest-ranking cabinet officials knew about it?

Throat surgery followed by counselling had been a quick and dirty solution, not just for her, but for all the singers in the project, all seven of them.

The only thing she had left was Eric and she clung to him like a life-raft.

She'd spent the not so generous payoff within the first year, on a university course, thinking education would stand her in good stead on the job market, but she was forty-four. Her first degree was years ago, and she was only trained to punch holes in things with her voice. After a year, she'd given up and found a job with the perks of cold pizza, and this was probably as good as it was going to get.

It was hardly fair.

Peter had no reason to get up but he gravitated towards the normal family-type sounds soon after Julie had sorted out Wayne. Breakfast was on the table, eggs and toast, a good meal in these hard times when many households made do with 'Nutrabrek' or one of the other brands of soy porridge which was cheap and filling and flavoured with God-knows-what to make it palatable. He still had a little of the cash which he had managed to bring with him and the whole family ate well enough at the moment, but he'd watched his balance dwindle frighteningly fast. He knew he had to find another job soon, Julie's wage would hardly support the children, let alone him as well.

Darren and Wayne were bickering as usual, and Ruby was sulking as she spooned egg into Dean's mouth. Peter knew that she and Julie had been arguing again. He'd heard the raised voices, but wisely kept out of yet another mother-daughter fight.

He felt a stab of regret that he had never been as close to his children as he might have been. His money had bought them ponies, and ballet lessons at the best school, but he had never been a full-time father to them. Now there was no going back.

His arrival quietened the boys for a moment and Julie shot him a grateful look.

"Good morning."

"Good morning." He dropped a light kiss on her bottle blonde hair.

Ten minutes later he separated Darren and Wayne for the third time and began to lay down the law. "Wayne, bathroom. Get washed. Now! Darren, find your shoes, its time for school."

Julie looked tired, she always looked tired until her face was painted on ready for work. Then for a few brief hours she sparkled. Life hadn't been easy bringing up four kids alone, but she'd managed somehow. All were the children of different fathers, and only Ruby was the product of something more than a casual union, but Peter didn't feel as though he had the right to pry into her past life since she was so careful not to pry into his.

"I'll take the boys to school this morning," he volunteered, "You look as though you could do with another couple of hours in bed."

She smiled at him, pretty despite the traces of last night's makeup around her eyes. He leaned over and kissed her again. Sometimes Julie looked so brittle he feared she might shatter.

"Get a room, guys." Ruby flounced out of the apartment, school bag over her shoulder.

Julie shrugged, "I don't know how to deal with her lately. She's growing up too fast. Perhaps she'll listen to you."

"Don't look at me, lady. Your daughter is nearly a woman and I was never very good at understanding women! Besides, I'm half your trouble. She sees me as a rival for your attention."

"No. I've seen the way she looks at you when she thinks I'm not watching. She sees me as the rival!"

"She's only twelve!"

"Not in her head."

"Perhaps I ought to have a talk with her then. I'm no one's ideal man."

"Except mine."

"Don't rely on me. I might not always be here."

"I know. I won't."

But she was beginning to and he knew it.

He dropped the boys off at school on his way to the jobshop. Of course, there was nothing available, so he decided to call in at some of the local clubs on the way home to see if they needed a piano player.

Five hours later, weary and dispirited, he headed back past the University and across the green expanse of Woodhouse Moor towards The Square. Those clubs big enough to employ resident musicians were all impressed with his musical abilities, but not in a position to offer him work. As he approached the tunnel that led into The Square, he fancied that he caught the strains of a melody which sounded familiar. One of his own songs from his early days, a song not as well known as most of his more recent work.

He stopped and looked around, but the singer was nowhere in sight, though in the distance a tall dark-skinned man was standing as if waiting for someone. Peter shrugged off the notion that he was being watched. He didn't think that the Bureau would be able to find him here, but he filed away the image of the black man for future consideration.

Over the next few weeks, he saw the man again a number of times. Occasionally he heard snatches of the tune and sometimes the tune and the man would coincide, but Peter was never close enough to check if the man was the singer. After a while he began to feel less uncomfortable. If the man was shadowing him, he would have done something by now. Gradually the man began to nod a neighbourly good morning as they passed each other in the Quadrangle. Peter relaxed again.

Maggie watched the black man from the balcony outside her apartment and memory supplied a name, Ives. He was a Singer. Why would they send a Singer to watch her now when all that was in her past? Her hand rested briefly on her throat. She was no danger to anyone. She was bound by the papers she had signed, and bound too by the certain knowledge that if she stepped out of line, Eric would lose his job and no door would open for either of them again.

Ruby pushed a hot mug of coffee into her hand.

"Come in, Maggie, it's cold with that door open," she said.

"The sun's shining now. You come out. You spend too much of your time indoors."

There was no answer, so Maggie stepped back in to the apartment. "You're too scared someone's going to report you to school, aren't you? Don't think you've taken me in. I know you shouldn't be here. If your mother knew where you were you'd be in a whole heap of trouble."

"She wouldn't care. She did the same as me when she was young."

"And look where she ended up. Don't you go thinking that she wants you to make the same mistakes as she did. It's more than likely that she expects you to learn by what happened to her."

Ruby didn't want to hear any more and she got up to go, but Maggie held her back.

"If you're going, child, you can do a favour for me and tell me what that man in the courtyard is doing."

"Which man?"

"Down there, hanging about near the tunnel. Tall black man in a leather jacket."

Ruby went out to the balcony and hung over the edge, trying to see.

"Oh yes. I can see him. Good looking isn't he? Is he a detective, Maggie? Are they after you for something?"

"No. He's no detective. I used to work in his line of business once. But I don't know what he wants, now."

"I'll watch him for you." She giggled, "It will be exciting, watching the watcher!" And with that she was gone.

Ives was there the following day, and the one after that. He hung around in the courtyard, though never looking up towards the apartment. Occasionally Maggie caught the snatch of a song. So Ives could still sing could he? Maggie's bitterness twisted inside her.

Singing, ordinary singing, not the kinetic kind, had been her greatest pleasure. She hadn't croaked a note for years. Experimentally she hummed a snatch of a nursery song. The notes in her head were not the ones that came out of her mouth, but the tune rose and fell in more or less the right places She grimaced and tried it again. Her voice trembled and the tune wobbled, but it was almost recognisable.

But not good enough.

Even so, Maggie found herself humming a tuneless little tune while she did household chores. Excitement rose within her. They'd made her believe it would be impossible, but it was not!

Did she still have the power? Could she still sing the songs of unmaking? Did she even want to? Not now. Her throat was hurting already with the unaccustomed usage. She was out of condition, but she would practise and maybe someday she would see if she could still deliver the goods.

The next day Ives was there again and Maggie's curtains twitched as she watched him from her window. He never looked up, but she could feel his continuous presence. He was like an itch she couldn't scratch. Why was he watching, waiting? Why? What had she done? She'd played by the rules. They didn't need to keep tabs on her, unless... did they know?

Suddenly he moved. It all happened so quickly that Maggie didn't register it at first. By the time she realised that he was moving he had disappeared out of her range of vision into the shadow of her block. They did know. This was it! He was coming for her. They knew she'd tried singing again. Maybe the apartment was wired.

Which way should she run? Blood pounded in her ears. If she was going to face Ives she wanted to do it out in the open, not here in her lonely apartment. She ran to the door, along the balcony and down the flights of stairs expecting at any moment to meet Ives coming up. Her breath came in rough gasps as she arrived at the bottom and ran out into the Square. Ives was not there, she turned and collided with someone. They fell in a tangle of bodies.

"Are you all right?" The stranger jumped to his feet quickly, reaching down to help her up. He was Ruby's latest uncle. She felt thoroughly embarrassed.

"Are you all right?" he repeated.

She held out her hand and he helped her to her feet. "Yes I think so. Are you? I'm sorry it was my fault!"

That's all right. My fault too. You're Mrs Burrows aren't you, Ruby's friend?"

"Maggie," she said.

"I'm Peter Beck. "

He was polite and friendly and not what Maggie had expected of one of Julie's boyfriends. She tried to pull her flustered senses together and look at him while checking her peripheral vision for Ives.

"Ruby's told me all about you," he said.

The kid talked too much. What had she said? Maggie focused at last on Ruby's Uncle Peter.

Peter Beck. Maggie had not recognised the name or the face, but she had worked with Singers for long enough to catch the trace of talent. Peter Beck had not been with the Department, Maggie had known all of the Singers there. He claimed to be Canadian, but Maggie had a good ear for accents and she was sure he was American. They had a project along similar lines to the British, but of course better funded and better equipped. If Beck was from their Bureau perhaps he was involved in all this.

Maggie shivered and felt the prickle of sweat on her forehead and between her breasts.

Peter was on the verge of leaving.

The cramped apartment was getting unbearable. He still hadn't been able to find a permanent job, though there had been occasional gigs which had brought in a little money. There was no longer enough to keep him supplied with Oblivion, and booze was no substitute for the total escape which the oil provided. He'd argued with Julie when she'd bought him a bottle with her overtime money and then he'd used it up within the week. When he'd come round from his binge and realised that there was only Nutrabrek on the table his guilt had led to more rows.

He was going to have to leave. Without a man in the house, Julie could at least apply for a state subsistence allowance for the kids. It wouldn't be much, but it would help.

He felt guilty about Julie too. He taken her shelter and comfort and given her nothing in return. He had nothing to give. There was no love; though he was genuinely fond of her. She'd begun to rely on him for advice and support, but she needed someone permanent and that wasn't him. He should leave now and give her chance to find another man, someone more reliable than him.

Maybe he'd try Manchester or Liverpool. London was too risky; his face was still too recognisable by those in the know. He should have had plastic surgery while he had the chance. Damn! There were lots of things he should have done.

Maggie watched Ives cross the Square. She hadn't seen Beck since that day when she had recognised him for what he was, but Ives had waited every day for weeks without making an approach of any kind. Each day that passed added insult to injury. He became the symbol of her rejection.

She stood in the middle of the kitchen and relaxed her shoulders. Breathe in—slowly. Slowly. Feel the diaphragm working. Now out. Control it, Use the muscles not the throat. Slowly—and relax. Good! The control was beginning to return. Muscles that had hardly been used in the last three years were gradually toning up. The notes were coming slowly and she had a range of about an octave. Not a patch on the three octaves she used to be able to sing, but it was improving. Her tone was rough, but her projection was stronger. She would Sing again!

Peter had become used to the presence of the black man around the buildings. He saw him often when he went to and from the apartment, and yesterday, on one of Peter's rare trips to the pub, he'd been there. They'd shared a companionable drink.

Peter had rowed with Julie again and he was in no hurry to return, so he gave the man, Ives, more time than he would normally spend with a stranger. When Ives turned out to be a fellow musician they began to talk shop. The pub was ancient, built in the late 1880s and deliberately preserved as a period piece. It still had a genuine upright piano standing proudly in what had been its Concert Room. Ives planted the idea and, after several drinks and encouragement from the landlord and the locals, Peter tried the keyboard, finding its touch a little strange, but at least it was in tune.

He played and when the crowd joined in he played a selection of songs until he found the musical era which best suited his audience—about twenty years behind the times, but that wasn't surprising. Through the mob of voices, Ives rich bass reached not only Peter's ears but his brain as well. There was something about the man's voice.

The pub landlord was happy. People had popped in for a drink and they'd stayed, spending far more over the bar than they normally did.

"When's he here again then?" One of the locals had nodded towards Peter, and that enquiry had prompted the offer of a job. It was only three evenings a week, but the money was regular and the tips were good.

He postponed his plans to leave.

Ives turned up the first night, and again on the second. Peter began to get used to his voice. The two men developed an easy friendship. Peter played and Ives sang and the audience loved it. The landlord let them use the pub room in the mornings to rehearse. Ives would bring songs written on scraps of paper and Peter would arrange them to suit the primitive piano.

"How about this one?" Ives pushed some creased sheet music in front of Peter's nose one day. "It's an old Hero Young song. I haven't heard it in ages, but I think it'll go down well. It could do with a harmony here and here." He pointed, "How about giving it a try? Your voice can't be that bad."

Peter stiffened and stared at the sheet music. 'Homeland'. It was the song of his unmaking. He closed the piano lid and stood up.

"You can still do it you know." Ives said softly, "It doesn't have to end in death or destruction!"

"Who are you? Are you from the Bureau?"

"No, my friend. They aren't as patient as I am. I'm independent. A free agent!"

"Leave me alone!"

The singalongs stopped. Peter told the landlord he was too sick to work. In reality he was too scared. Maybe not of Ives—if the man had meant him any harm he wouldn't have waited this long—but of himself.

Ives took to waiting in the Square all day and Peter had to walk past him whenever he went out, so he stopped going out. Ruby ran all his errands for him. He sat all day in the apartment, alone with his thoughts. Stay, go. Go, stay. Even Julie couldn't get through his moodiness and in the end she stopped trying.

"He's there again." Ruby told Maggie. "I've been watching him for hours. He never moves. He's right down by your block entrance, staring out over the Square."

"What does he want with me? Why doesn't he make a move?"

Maggie stared at the shadowy figure from a distance and hate bubbled inside her. Mind games! The department was good at that. Had he heard her practising? She knew that trained Singers tended to be able to pick up frequencies from some distance away. Perhaps some of their other decommissioned singers had started to sing again too. Maggie grinned without humour. Her range had increased by another half octave. Soon she would try the song of unmaking.

The money had run out again. It wouldn't have been so bad, but the expected rent rise had finally come and Peter could ignore his conscience no longer. He had to go down to the jobshop, or leave to allow Julie to put in her subsistence claim. If the office suspected there was a man here Julie would be banned from drawing benefits for life, even if she starved.

The jobshop was full of no-hopers. He signed on as a labourer first, do anything, go anywhere, and as a musician as his alternative. There was nothing in either category.

Outside the jobshop Peter walked straight into Ives.

"Are you following me?" Peter asked.

"We've got to talk."

"I've got nothing to say."

"Then listen."

Peter walked ahead quickly, but Ives kept pace with him.

"We know all about you, Hero Young. We know how the US Bureau forced you into testing and we have a copy of those test results."

Peter slowed down and Ives continued. "The Bureau is still looking for you. They arranged the reports of your death. Your family believes it. If the Bureau finds you, it might as well be true."

"And who are you working for if it's not them? Are you with the British?"

"I was until five years ago. I ran a few weeks before they pulled the plug on the whole scheme. I work for an independent firm now."

"Independent or some other government?"

"Independent! Truly independent. We work for the highest bidder as long as we like the job. We can pick and choose, we're a pretty unique outfit."

"And you want me."

"We need you. And you need us."

"Mercenaries?"

"It's not like that. We're civilian. Working for the military is by choice, and your politics are your own affair."

"But some do?"

"Occasionally—if the money's good or the cause is just. I told you, the work you choose to accept is your own affair."

"A dangerous concept, killing in a good cause."

The expression on the boffin's face before he exploded into his component molecules would be with Peter forever.

"No one will force anything on you."

"Are you legitimate?"

"Well, we don't file tax returns, if that's what you mean, but we don't break the laws of common decency either. Look, Peter..." He grabbed Peter's arm and brought him to a standstill. "I certainly can't promise that it will always be safe. But I can say that the rewards will be in proportion to the risks. The third world is changing rapidly and there are governments out there that are very accommodating."

"I won't risk lives."

"That choice is yours, but don't forget that it takes training to use your talent safely. Once trained, your skills can be used to good effect for peaceful purposes. Do you know how many men it takes to carve out a mile of new road in Nepal? Or how long it takes to drill for water in the desert? With the right kind of training, you can use your kinetic energy for specific purposes. You can learn to control it so that it doesn't kill again. Please tell me you'll think about it."

Peter didn't say no.

Eric was dead and Maggie's life was in ruins. Last week he had been alive and well and then a virus, a cough, pneumonia; three days in the community ward of the local hospital and he was gone. It said pneumonia and sepsis on the death certificate. Maggie stared at the rent rise notification. It was addressed to her, rather than him. Records were altered super-efficiently, with indecent haste.

There was no way she could afford this apartment now. Her wage wouldn't even meet the old rent. She was still going through the motions, living out a life which had become meaningless to her without Eric. A few years ago, she would have been able to afford the emergency treatment that might have saved his life.

Now he was gone. But if it hadn't been for the Department axing her project she would have had the money to save him.

The Department. Ives! What did he want? If he was going to offer her a job he was too damned late.

She began to throw clothes into a suitcase, forcing her trembling hands to fumble with the catches until they clicked. That solid sound marked the end of everything she had ever known. She had stripped down her possessions to the meagre amount she would be allowed space for in a hostel. Tears ran down her face, shining black rivers in an ocean of despair.

"You're leaving." Ruby was in the doorway behind her. "He's leaving too."

"Who?"

"My Hero!"

"Your Uncle Peter?"

"Don't call him that! He's not my uncle. None of them have ever been real uncles!"

"Don't take it out on me. " Maggie snapped back automatically then regretted it but she was too sunk in her own misery to offer much consolation. "I thought you wanted him to leave. You've always been glad before."

"He's different."

"Your Mum has thought that about each and every one of them, but they all turned out the same in the end."

"Mum's not crying this time. Usually she weeps buckets and then finds another man, but this time she's sitting quiet while he tells her how she'll be better off without him and how he'll send some money back when he's saved some from this new job. He's going abroad somewhere. He'll never come back—he hasn't even promised that he will. They usually do when she gets upset."

"Are you going to go and say goodbye?"

"No."

"You can see me off then. This rent rise has finished me. I'm going to a hostel."

"Take me with you."

"How can I do that? I think they'd suspect you're not my daughter!"

Ruby's eyes were full of unshed tears. So the kid wasn't as hard as she made out to be. Maggie had suspected her of all sorts of slyness in the past, but now she felt pity. The girl was hurt and confused, too old to be a child and too young to be an adult. She stood there in a thin dress that was far too small for her and Maggie knew that this pathetic figure was the only person who would miss her.

Here, take this. I can't take it with me and I don't want to leave it for strangers." She held out a figurine in delicate porcelain. A girl with a goose. "It's real old. It belonged to Eric's grandmother."

"You could have sold it for the rent money."

"Money runs out when you've spent it, but something like this will last forever. There isn't enough beauty in this world. Now, child, I'm all packed. Run down and tell me if that Department man is still there.

She left the front door unlocked, the key in it, ready for the next occupant. As she walked away from her memories, she began to sob convulsively, her round face contorted.

In the courtyard, there was no immediate sign of Ives, but within three paces she spotted him across the Square, walking towards her briskly. He must know she was leaving. What now? His pace didn't increase as he drew closer, but Maggie's panic began to mount. The sobbing turned to hysterics and Ives became the focus for all her grief and frustration. He became the Department, the man with the power, the cause of all her trouble. Something snapped. She began to scream.

Peter left Julie in the apartment. He carried a single battered bag slowly down the steps without looking back. Between the first and second landing he heard the commotion below. A woman shrieked abuse. Ives voice was there, reasoning and calm, but the woman was yelling and sobbing.

Peter ran to the front of the first-floor balcony and looked down. It was Ruby's friend, Maggie. She was struggling against the grip of several neighbours, trying to get at Ives who was plainly out of his depth. Peter heard him ask what all the fuss was about, and the woman, her voice still raised in frenzy yelled, "If you've come to find out if I can still Sing then the answer is 'Yes!' But you'll never get me back into the Department now. NEVER!"

She began to Sing, a cracked contralto voice, but Peter recognised the power in it.

He dropped his bag and started to run. The sound was all around him, pulsing with a life of its own. His head ached and his ears rang. Down in the Square the neighbours had released Maggie and were staggering back, holding their hands over their ears to block out the destructive waves of kinetic sound.

Maggie reached the top of her comfortable range and changed gear into a sweeping crescendo. The ground began to rumble and shake and the fabric of the buildings slowly began to disintegrate. Masonry crashed down in the courtyard. Peter looked up in horror as the top of the building began to ripple like waves on a beach.

Peter heard Ives join in with a harmony and the two voices blended into one sound. The frequencies changed and Peter saw the building begin to stabilise for a moment. Ives' voice was strong and sure, but Peter sensed that it wasn't enough.

Secondary shock waves began to hit the building. Ives didn't stop singing, but he motioned for Peter to join in. It needed another note to flesh out the chord. To turn the song into a song of 'Making'.

Peter stood transfixed. The neighbours were all on the ground now. Only Ives and the Maggie stood, Singing at each other across the moaning bodies while the building still crumbled about them. Ives had said that Singing could be used for good. This destruction had to be stopped. Peter knew it, but something held him back.

He wasn't even sure if he could find the right note. If he chose the wrong harmony he would bring the whole world crashing down on top of them. Should it be major or minor, harmonic or discordant? He daren't Sing, but he daren't keep silence either.

He found a note, a fourth below the tonic and joined in. The stones fell faster and quickly he backed off and changed the harmony, moving to a third above. His voice rose in intensity as he realised that his second choice had been correct. He called upon memory to take his voice into the realms where it had only travelled once before.

He was out of condition. The muscles of his ribcage protested and cramped and his vision clouded, but he managed to keep the note even and strong. It mattered now more than it had ever mattered on stage. The three voices blended into a chord and the world steadied. Maggie's voice tailed off and she stepped back, dazed at the havoc she had caused. All over the Square rubble was littered and people stood, speechless with disbelief.

"It must have been an earthquake." One voice hazarded a guess and they all mumbled assent.

"Ruby!" Julie's voice was shrill and hysterical, coming from the balcony above.

"Ruby! Oh my God! Ruby!"

Peter looked to where she was staring and he felt all the breath leave his body. From beneath a pile of rubble he could see a child's hand reaching for a perfect porcelain figure, the girl with the goose, lay undamaged.

And the child?

Julie ran past him and he reached towards her, but Maggie's shriek froze his movement.

"Dear Heaven, not the child too. It should have been me." Maggie lurched into the access tunnel.

Peter felt the ground shudder as the song began again. His first instinct was to go after her, but Ives grabbed his arm.

"This one's a solo," he said softly. "Besides—" He nodded to where Julie was hunched over Ruby's tomb.

"She's here!" Julie yelled. "Help me."

Stung that his first thought had been to help Maggie before Ruby, Peter turned. Steering Julie out of the way by her shaking shoulders, he strained to lift a jagged block of concrete. Ives bent to help, and between them they managed to tip it sideways and slide it away, crushing the goose-girl statue to powder under its weight. Beneath the block, nestled in a tiny cave, Ruby, face grey with dust, twitched and coughed.

"Ruby!" Julie dropped to her knees and grabbed the child's hand to pull her free.

Behind them, Maggie's song ended in the roar of falling blocks.

When the dust had settled, Ives touched Peter's shoulder. "We go now."

"Not yet." Peter looked over to Julie and Ruby.

"You can't stay. How long do you think it will take the Brits to realise that Leeds is outside the earthquake zone? Your own Bureau will make the connection, too and they'll have a team here soon after that. Three hours at the outside. You'll be no use to Julie then. And what will the Bureau make you into?"

"Three hours you reckon?"

"At the outside."

"Long enough to make sure they're all right. I'll meet you in two."

Ives studied Peter's face for a moment and nodded.

"Don't be late."

*Jacey Bedford writes fantasy and science fiction, she's been published on both sides of the Atlantic. Her seven books (so far) are published by DAW: **Empire of Dust**, **Crossways**, and **Nimbus**, Psi-Tech novels. (Science fiction/space opera.), plus the Rowankind Trilogy: **Winterwood**, **Silverwolf** and **Rowankind** (Historical fantasy set in 1800 with a cross-dressing female privateer captain, a jealous ghost, and a wolf shapechanger.) Followed by a standalone historical fantasy, **The Amber Crown***

Maiden of the Rock

Holley Cornetto

Liam first dreamt of the maiden of the rock fourteen years ago, the same year his mother died. He could still remember the exhilaration that first time he saw her, bare-breasted and impossibly beautiful, sitting on her rock. Around her were miles of open water, dull beneath the lead-gray sky. She was alone, as alone as his mother had been.

From that night on, her face haunted him. Her eyes shone out through the bleak nothingness, a beacon of light softening the harshness of the sea. He was sure she was real, certain she was out there somewhere, waiting for him to find her.

As the years passed, Liam found himself dreaming more and more often of the maiden of the rock. Some nights she sat staring out to sea, as if she saw more than the turquoise waves pressing in around her. Other nights she sang, and the sea stilled to listen to her melancholy song. It was because of those dreams that he vowed to find her, to rescue her from her prison in the middle of the sea.

He wasn't crazy. He'd spent the twenty years following his mother's death watching ships by the harbor. Mixed in among the small fishing boats were clippers, schooners, and frigates. He knew the name of every ship, and who captained each. Local sailors who heard of his tragedy took pity on him, telling him stories of life on the open sea, the places they traveled, and people they'd met. He heard stories of adventures, of sea monsters and pirates, but his favorite tales were of the maiden of the rock. Sailors whispered of her beauty. With her strawberry hair and sun kissed skin, she could charm even the hardest of hearts. Although they spoke of her in reverend tones, they warned that seeing her often meant death.

As Liam got older, his habits changed. He spent less time haunting the harbor, and more time researching the maiden of the rock. He read every book, visited every library, and followed every lead he could find, no matter how far-fetched they seemed. He still sought out news from sailors, but did so by frequenting taverns near the wharf, buying drinks for sailors and captains alike in exchange for their tales. He questioned them until they lost patience or were too drunk to answer.

His favorite tavern was The Anchor. The place served watered down swill passed off as ale and was always full of men fresh from the harbor. A musky odor hung heavy in the air. Raucous laughter broke out on the opposite side of the room as two drunken sailors shoved each other and traded insults. Shadows grew longer as the sun began to set, and the lamplighters went about their work.

"But surely there is honor in naval service? What of the tales I've heard on the docks?" He slammed his fist on the bar top, animated by too much drink.

"Those days have passed." Saunders, the old captain stared at the bottom of his empty glass. "These days, most sailors are little better than pirates. They wreak havoc in every port, leaving broken inns and bastard children in their wake. It is no life of honor. It's the life of a man who has nothing, and who never will."

Saunders didn't have a ship, hadn't even captained a vessel since his days on The Odyssey, but he'd been patient and kind to Liam, especially in the years after his mother passed. He was the only man for the job. Liam plunked a canvas pouch, heavy with coins, on the counter beside the old captain.

Saunders looked around in a panic and shoved the heavy pouch back towards him. "Are you crazy, boy? Put that away. You come in here waving around a sack of coins like that and you're bound to get us both killed."

Liam sheepishly slid the pouch into his lap. "I apologize. I want… I need your help."

Saunders tilted his head. "Go on."

"I want to hire you. I bought a ship, and I need a crew."

The old man doubled over in laughter and slapped his knee. "Landlubber like you? Want to captain a ship, do ya?"

"No, no. I don't want to captain the ship. I want *you* to captain the ship."

"Oiy, and why would I do such a thing?"

"I'll pay you. I'll pay you well. And, after the voyage is over. After I've gotten… found… what I'm looking for. After that, I'll give you the ship."

The mirth faded from the old captain's face. "Why don't you just hire a ship and crew? Why buy your own, if you'll just be rid of it when you're done?"

Liam looked around the tavern. There were too many people here. Someone would overhear him, and they might try to get to her first. She sat there, night after night, waiting for him. He'd be damned if someone else got there first. "There is something I need to find."

Saunders scoffed. "Buried treasure?"

Liam shook his head. "I'll tell you, but not here."

Saunders nodded. "We can talk in my room."

The room reminded Saunders of being at sea. The smell of fish and piss had soaked into the furniture and walls. A thin, slimy film covered every surface. It was the cheapest pit in town, and soon he wouldn't be able to afford it.

The little oil lamp was enough to light the cramped space -- just as well, as he couldn't afford candles. He crossed his arms over his chest. "Now, tell me what's so important that you'd buy a ship."

"You'll think me mad."

He guffawed. "I already think you're mad, laddy. You must expect a big haul, because that's a hell of a lot of money to throw away on one trip. If you want me to captain this little expedition of yours, I need to know what I'm getting myself into. So, tell me why you won't just hire out a ship and crew."

"No one would sign on."

"Why?"

"Because I don't know for certain where she is."

"She?" Saunders took his pipe from the table.

"She's out there, somewhere."

Saunders lit his pipe and took a long pull.

"...Lorelei."

Saunders choked. "The maiden of the rock? She's led a thousand men to their deaths."

"You know of her?"

"Every sailor knows that old yarn." Saunders leaned back in his chair and began to recite:

"One by one they come to die,
All the grooms of Lorelei.
She drags them down into the sea,
Where they remain eternally.
Then she returns to watch and wait,
Until another takes the bait."

Liam shook his head. "It isn't true. She's not like that. She wants me to find her. She chose me"

At least the kid was honest. Mad, certainly, but there was something to be said for his forthrightness. "I can't take your coin, boy. She's a legend. An old wives' tale, and looking for her is not only folly, it's likely to get you killed."

"My mind is set in this. I want you to captain my vessel."

"You want me to deliver you unto death. I can't conscience it."

"That is precisely why I need you."

Saunders shook his head, taking another puff of his pipe. "There are hundreds of seamen in this town. Why ask me?"

Liam smiled. "Because I've heard stories about you since I was a kid. About what happened on The Odyssey. You held fast; you stayed true to your mission. You could have made a fortune, but duty and honor were more important to you."

Saunders smirked. "You make me sound like a hero for doing my job."

"When doing your job is the hard thing, perhaps. See, if I were to hire just anyone, I'd find a man for the job. He'd sail the ship to and fro, chasing the wind, but never actually looking for her. Or, perhaps he'd try and take her for himself. But not Captain Benjamin Saunders. He would try in earnest to help me find her, because he believes in duty and honor."

The truth of it was that he needed the boy's coin. He knew the maiden wasn't real, but he'd take the job, even if he thought Liam mad. It was like stealing. Not stealing, he told himself, a job. He'd be paid for services rendered.

He nodded and scratched his scruffy beard. "When would you like to depart?"

"As soon as possible, but I've had trouble pinpointing her location. You've sailed these waters for years; do you know where to find her?"

Saunders shrugged. "Same as every legend, every tale. She exists everywhere and nowhere. Might be impossible to track down the origins of the rhyme. What if we can't find her?"

"We set a date, and if we've found nothing by then, the ship and the payment are yours."

It was madness, but he knew if he didn't agree, the boy would hire someone else. Someone who would take advantage of him and rob him of his coin. At least I'll keep an eye on him, Saunders thought. I'll keep him out of trouble, let him experience the sea. He'll have a story, something to tell his grandkids someday. Finally, he offered Liam his hand. "Very well, lad. As you say."

The boy looked relieved. "You can hire the crew. Whoever you like, your choice."

Saunders nodded. He'd expected as much. One look at the boy's hands told him that Liam knew nothing of the sea, of hard labor. This would be an easy enough job, he figured. Most likely, they'd just sail around until the boy got tired and wanted to return to land.

Saunders sighed. He was going to have a hell of a time hiring a crew when he had no idea where they were going.

Liam knew from the start that the voyage would be a long one, or at least he should have. Since they'd set sail, his dreams of the maiden grew more frequent. It was as if, somehow, she knew he was coming for her.

At first, he spent most of his time on deck with Saunders and the crew, watching the sea as if his maiden might be just over the horizon.

With its endless rolling waves, the sea made him feel small. It reminded him of being a boy, and of his mother. They'd spent many afternoons together on the beach, collecting shells and leaving footprints in the sand. His mother had loved the sea, so he had loved it also.

But, after nine weeks had passed, the excitement faded.

Life at sea was nothing like he'd expected. He thought they'd face pirates and find adventure, but the truth was, they faced nothing but miles of vast, open sea. Once they'd spotted dolphins swimming in the ship's wake, but that had only provided an afternoon's entertainment.

After weeks of finding nothing, Liam stopped coming above deck. Instead, he spent his days shuffling through the pages of notes he'd made about Lorelei.

The first time he visited the library, he'd shown his sketch to the librarian, and the man brought him an armful of books he could barely see over.

The librarian opened one of the books, an encyclopedic tome, and flipped through the pages. Each page had an illustration, accompanied by text. A bestiary, the librarian said, as if his beautiful, perfect Lorelei were a beast. A creature. An animal.

The librarian pointed to an image labeled Undine and pushed the book towards Liam.

The picture didn't capture any of her beauty, her magic. The woman on the rock looked inhuman, like a monster. Her hair was tangled seaweed, her mouth a sinister grin of sharpened teeth. There was nothing there of his angelic Lorelei, the one who called to him with her song.

But the thing that bothered him most was her face. The face in the book was wrong.

Though Liam copied down all he could find on undines, he remained skeptical of his sources. The book had called his Lorelai a beast, after all. It said she lacked a soul, which he knew to be false. He had glimpsed her soul; she bared it to him through her song. A song that had always been eerily familiar to him.

#

Saunders knocked at the cabin door. Since Liam had financed the trip, he had taken private quarters for himself.

"Come in."

He pushed open the door. The boy sat at his makeshift desk, shuffling his papers again. These days, it was how he spent most of his time. He had books, sketches, maps, scraps of song lyrics, and bawdy rhymes. Any hint or rumor Liam had ever heard was collected in those notes, or so he said. The walls of the cabin were lined in sketches of her from every angle. They all had the same face, a face that seemed familiar. But perhaps he'd just seen the pictures too many times.

"We're going to have to make for port soon, lad, or else we're going to run out of provisions."

Liam brought his hand down hard on the desk, scattering his collection of papers. "No! Not when we're so close." Dark crescents ringed his eyes. He'd lost weight. Too much.

"There's talk among the crew. If we don't turn it in soon, we may not have a choice. We only brought enough rations for the eight weeks as we agreed, and they ain't gonna last much longer. We should be heading back to port, while we still have enough to get there."

"Captain, can you not control your men?"

Saunders sighed. "I've kept up my end." This was a fool's errand to begin with. Surely the boy could see that by now.

"It's Driscoll, isn't it? I can hear him at night, pacing the decks, ranting at anyone who'll listen. He's loud, I'll grant that, but the men don't have faith in him. Silence him, and the rest of the men will fall in line and see the job done."

"There is no 'done.' There will be no end to this because she doesn't exist. She's a fairy story, made up by sailors too long out to sea."

Liam shook his head. "She is real, she--"

There was a crash outside the door, accompanied by the sounds of men shouting and running. "Captain! Captain! Get out here!"

He started for the door. "We'll finish this later."

A thick fog had rolled in, masking the endless gray waves. The air was dense with a mist that hovered just above the deck. Gray on gray, the sky and the sea felt eerily as one. Saunders turned. "For God's sake, what is it?"

"Sir," said a crewman just out of sight. "Listen."

Saunders paused. He closed his eyes, breathing in the thick air. Over the creaking of the ship and crashing waves, he heard the ghostly echo of a woman's voice.

"I'll be damned right to hell."

"Do you hear it, sir?"

"Yes! Yes, I hear it. The question is, what in the bloody hell is it?"

"It's her…"

Saunders turned to see Liam standing above deck for the first time in weeks.

Driscoll spat in Liam's direction. "Like hell it is. It's the storm. Wind on the waves."

"You hear it. You all hear it! We're close." Liam's eyes were wide and half-crazed.

Whispers crept like shadows between the men on deck. They had all signed on, some believing they might find the maiden of the rock, others less sure, but eager for the coin - half up front, and half when the ship returned. Men like Driscoll.

Saunders knew this was the last chance. He looked from Liam to his crew. "We sail toward it, whatever it is. If we don't find it in three days, we head for the nearest port."

"And when we find her," Liam added, "I'll throw in a bonus for every man on board!"

A cheer went up among the crew. All but Driscoll, who slunk below deck while the others cheered.

The dreams came every night. Sometimes Lorelei was the maiden on the rock, perfection made flesh. Other times, she was the monster from the bestiary, with seaweed hair, and teeth like a shark's. The closer they got, the more vivid the dreams became. It was how he knew they were close.

Saunders had been a fool to suggest turning away, but Liam could hardly blame him. He hadn't understood before, but now… now they'd heard her sing. Even Driscoll wouldn't be able to deny her existence any longer.

Liam tossed and turned in a restless fit. The fog and mist had crept in, coating every surface with damp. The scent of mildew wafted up from the ship's hold. He closed his eyes and sank into the oblivion of sleep.

He could feel the murky seabed on his feet, and wetness on his cheeks. This time, when he dreamed, it was not of Lorelei, but of his mother. He watched as they pulled her bloated purple corpse from the fishing nets. Drowned. That was her official cause of death. No one knew what she'd been doing in the water or how she'd gotten there, and none cared enough to ask. But the dream was wrong, because in it, he was an adult. He'd been a child when they found his mother's body. He stood on the beach, barefooted, with sand squelching between his toes. Tiny crabs scuttled towards him and back, as if beckoning him to follow them out to sea. "Come with us," he imagined them saying.

He blinked, and when he opened his eyes, he was in the apartment where he grew up. His mother was alive, somewhere just out of sight. She sang as she did the wash, her voice achingly familiar. He knew her song, knew it down to his bones, and yet couldn't place it.

Why couldn't he see her face?

Liam opened his eyes. He was back on the ship, standing above deck in his bedclothes. He couldn't remember how he'd gotten there. It was odd, he hadn't suffered a fit of somnambulism since he was a boy, the summer after they'd found his mother. He rubbed his eyes. He could still see the shape of her corpse, the shadow of his dream fading into the night. Part of the dream was true. He had been at the beach the day they pulled his mother's body out of the water.

His bare feet slid across the deck as he made his way back towards the hatch. He needed rest. Tomorrow, they'd find Lorelei.

Below deck, he paused at the sound of voices. Men arguing. He recognized Driscoll's voice and crept closer.

"We should head for port now. We'll run out of food!"

"Only three more days, then we go. Girl or no." It sounded like Saunders.

"There ain't no girl! She's a tale to explain sunken ships and men jumping overboard. The crew is gonna start jumping if you don't do something!"

"I am doing something. He's a good lad. We all know what happened to his mother when he was a boy. We give him three days, and then we turn back. He needs to make peace with the sea, after what it took from him."

"She was a whore, is what she was. She was out there selling her wares to any sailor with a coin to pay. That's how she ended up like she did. Hell, any one of us could be his father."

"Hush!" Saunders cut him off. "This ain't the time nor place."

Liam's blood ran cold. Saunders hadn't denied it. He racked his brain, trying to conjure memories of his mother. Always by the docks, leaving him on the beach to play while she... while she what?

After his mother died, it was as if she'd never even existed, as if he was the only one who remembered her or cared that she'd died. Liam was taken to his aunt. He had never visited her while his mother was alive. He hadn't even known he had an aunt. She gave him everything he could ask for, but she refused to talk about his mother.

Liam turned, sliding his hands along the wall in the dark, feeling his way back to his cabin. The wood was wet, slick and viscous. His stomach churned. He opened the cabin door and collapsed onto his bed, weeping long into the night.

Saunders tapped his pipe against the table, knocking the ash loose, shaking it out onto the floor. Another day had passed and they'd found nothing. He knew no matter what he said, the lad wouldn't be satisfied. He saw that now. He hadn't taken into account that Liam might still be grieving after all these years, but the sea had taken the boy's mother. What Liam was searching for, he'd never find. Not really, and Saunders would have to be the one to tell him.

His cabin door creaked as it swung open. "Captain?"

Saunders scowled. "I asked not to be disturbed."

The boy, Jon, stood stiff and pale. "I'm sorry, Sir. But, it's Driscoll."

"What about him?"

"We can't find him, Sir. We've searched the whole ship."

"We? Who else knows?"

"Only a few."

"Better not to raise a stir yet. He's probably catching a nap somewhere." Saunders pulled on his boots and headed above deck.

He joined Jon and the others in their search for Driscoll. The man could be volatile, but it wasn't like him to shirk his duties. After searching the ship a third time, he hung his head. He had no choice but to alert the crew. More than half a day had passed, and Driscoll's absence had already been noticed.

As the men gathered on the deck, Saunders inhaled deeply. The thick fog that set in yesterday had not lifted. Its presence added a certain layer of gloom to the atmosphere. "There ain't an easy way to say this, but Driscoll's gone missing. Has anyone had eyes on him since last night?"

Some of the men muttered. "We heard her singing again last night."

"It was her. It was the maiden of the rock!"

"She called him to sea!"

Saunders sighed. He'd heard the sound, but he still wasn't convinced. He'd hoped the men knew better, but most of them believed, or at least wanted to believe the stories.

"It was clear as a bell. We thought we found 'er. Driscoll was cursing, and looking out, but the fog was so thick nobody saw nothing."

"Where was he when you saw him last?"

"He was here, on the deck, making the rounds. Just before dawn."

"Uhm, captain?" One of the men stepped forward.

"Speak, sailor."

"Liam was above deck, too. About the same time..." he hesitated. "He was dressed in his nightclothes, sir. He had blood on his shirt. Said it was a nosebleed."

He frowned. Liam? Above deck? "I'll go talk to the lad. You all stay here. Keep searching, just in case. See if you see anything in the water."

Saunders scurried down the hatch and pounded at Liam's door.

A drowsy voice answered. "I'm not feeling well."

"I need to see you, boy. It won't keep."

There was a soft groan. Saunders took the spare key from his pocket and slid the door open.

Liam lay curled in a ball on his bed, his clothes a bloody mess.

"Hells, boy! What happened to you?"

"I don't know. I don't remember. I was asleep and then I woke up above deck. I thought I was dreaming. He told me she wasn't real. He told me that my mother, that she--" he broke off into a sob.

"Driscoll?"

Liam nodded.

"Oh, no. Tell me you didn't, boy. Please, tell me you didn't."

Liam held up his hands, covered in dried blood.

Liam sat in the dinghy, looking down at his basket of provisions. A half portion of food and water, and a pistol with one bullet. The crew wanted to hang him for Driscoll's murder, but Saunders talked them in to setting him adrift him instead.

"There ain't nothing but open sea for miles. He'll be good as dead, anyway. The boy's mad, not evil. He didn't mean to kill Driscoll; he was out of his mind."

<u>Out of his mind</u>.

He lifted the oars and began to row, heading in the direction that he'd last heard her voice. Lorelei was waiting for him. He rowed until his arms ached, then leaned back, letting the boat drift in the rocking waves as he closed his eyes to rest.

He woke to the sound of her voice. He'd been dreaming of his mother again. His mother twirling around their apartment, singing. Singing Lorelei's song. He ate what food remained, but rationed the water. His gaze fell on the pistol.

"Lorelei?" He took up the oars and rowed again, his arms aching from effort and exhaustion. He called again, and paused, waiting to hear an answer, her song, anything.

There was nothing. He slept.

The next time he opened his eyes, he saw a silhouette. A darkness that broke through the hazy evening fog. Her rock. It must be her rock. He picked up his oars and rowed hard. Waves like giant walls of water pushed his boat forward, as if the very sea itself willed him to find her. He dropped an oar as wood crashed against stone. Water spilled into the boat.

He dove in and circled the rock, but she wasn't there. There was nothing, no sign that she'd ever been there at all. He treaded water, the oppressiveness of the sea closing in around him. It was overwhelming, like being the only one who remembered his mother, trying desperately to keep that memory alive.

He was tired of trying. He stopped.

For a split second, he felt a sense of peace. He was a boy again, playing in the sand on the beach, waiting to hear the sound of his mother's voice, calling him home. As he descended, sinking deeper into the murky depths, a woman appeared beside him. Lorelei, the maiden of the rock. She took his hand and led him down into the unending deep.

The pressure grew, squeezing the air from his lungs. He was going to die, but at least he wouldn't die alone. As he smiled to thank the woman, he saw the delicate lines of her face. His mother's face.

Holley Cornetto *is a writer, librarian, professor, book reviewer, and transplanted southerner who now calls New Jersey home. Her debut novella, We Haunt These Woods, is available from Bleeding Edge Books. Her short fiction has appeared in magazines such as Daily Science Fiction, Flame Tree Press Newsletter, Dark Recesses Press, and several anthologies.In addition to writing The Horror Tree's weekly newsletter, she regularly reviews for Publisher's Weekly, Ginger Nuts of Horror, and The Horror Tree. She teaches creative writing in the online MFA program at Southern New Hampshire University. Find her on Twitter @HLCornetto.*

Coblyn

JL George

Myra's out front of Tesco when she sees it.

She's tired and overcaffeinated, a crawling feeling under the skin of her forearms and the back of her neck that's been there since Susan at work had that argument with Mr Wong just after lunch and strode into the back office fuming and swearing. Other people's anger always puts Myra on edge: however hard she tries to tune it out, it gets everywhere, like secondhand smoke. She fumbles with her phone to check her shopping list and swears as it catches first on the handle of her tote bag, then the loop on her umbrella.

A woman standing near the shop entrance side-eyes her. Myra's attention skates over her—dark circles under her eyes, a hollow-cheeked, harried look that might mean she's homeless, or just burned out. Sensible raincoat in that shade Myra's mum likes, British racing green; handbag from M&S. Something cradled in her arms.

The something is what draws Myra's gaze back. She thinks at first that it's a chihuahua, or one of those other breeds of yappy little dog—and then, ridiculously, a guinea pig.

But its face is furless, pinkish-grey and pinched around a hedgehoggy snout, and its eyes flat beetle-black, reflecting the shopfront red and blue. It clutches the woman's sleeve with a tiny hand. Elongated fingers like a monkey's. Light filters pink through its veined bat-ears.

Myra blinks a few times, hoping to dislodge the image of the thing, but it's still there. A puppet, must be, or a pet dressed up in a stupid costume for one of those Twitter accounts. *Dogs that look like Yoda* or some bollocks.

The thing lifts one miniature hand and extends it toward her. Opens its mouth, lined with needle-teeth, around a wordless noise. Dirt is rimed into the creases of its knuckles.

The woman looks down at it, scrunching up her face, and back at Myra. Caught staring, Myra takes an involuntary step back, lowers her eyes, but it's too late: the woman is already striding toward her.

Myra puts her hands up, fumbles for words to warn off whatever trouble she's invited. Waits for the inevitable, *What are you staring at?*

The woman thrusts it at her. Without Myra's say-so, her hands extend to take it. Instinct, the same way you wouldn't allow a baby or a pet to be dropped. It curls its fingers, furry and a little damp, around her thumb.

"What—" Myra starts to say, "I don't—". But the woman turns tail, pulling her green anorak tight around herself and fleeing down the street. Before Myra can follow her, she's lost among the after-work crowd.

The security guard loitering near the shop doorway is watching Myra. She turns to him, the creature still clutched in her arms awkwardly, like a colleague's baby that she didn't ask to hold. "Did you see that?" she demands. "What am I supposed to do with this?"

The security guard's hand goes to his radio. "Do with *what*?"

It clutches her upper arm when she tries to put it down. She twists around, shakes her shoulders, and it clings tighter. A mum with two school-age kids puts herself between them and Myra, herding them away. Myra stills as they skirt around her.

"Come on," she says—not to anyone in particular, casting desperately around for acknowledgement. Nobody meets her eyes. "Tell me you see this. You've got to see this!"

The guard sighs and plots over, looking put-upon at being forced to uproot himself from his spot by the door. "D'you need to ring someone, love?"

A couple of teenagers hanging around near the bins giggle nervously. One of them reaches for her phone.

"No," Myra says. "Thanks." She puts her head down and hurries away.

"Did you get milk?" Darren greets her when she gets home. He doesn't bat an eyelid at the creature.

"No," she huffs. "Tesco was a bit..." She trails off, holding it out as answer.

"A bit what?"

It obligingly shuffles around to cling to Myra's back while she unbuttons her coat, piggybacking there like a baby monkey. Its breath comes in warm, damp puffs against the back of her neck. "You really don't see it?"

His eyebrows draw together in the ten-past-ten vee of a cartoon frown. "Did you get your hair done?"

Myra frowns right back and blows a strand of fading blonde out of her face. "No."

It makes its way back over her shoulder to toy with the lanyard of her work ID. She yanks the lanyard off over her head and throws it onto the counter, where it skitters across the plastic top and comes to a halt against the spaghetti.

"Alright, alright," Darren says. "No need to throw a strop."

She opens her mouth to yell, to demand that he acknowledge it, and closes it again.

The security guard. The people outside the supermarket. Is it possible this is all in her head? Her mother always said she had an overactive imagination, that she'd say anything for attention. (The kids who stuck gum in her hair at school were only messing about; the teacher who'd offered her a lift home from netball practice and laid a heavy hand on her thigh in the car probably wasn't looking what he was doing.) Myra learned to second-guess herself, to accept that she was probably wrong.

Maybe this is more of the same.

Darren is still staring at her.

"Don't worry about it," she says. The creature purrs and nuzzles her cheek.

She tries shutting it out of the flat that night. Dumps it round back by the bin store and locks the door. Sometime in the night, she's woken by a dip of the mattress and the smell of rain and rubbish. Its weight settles on her chest, presses down on her breastbone as it wiggles to get comfortable.

She drives to the other side of town and kicks it out of the car, then tears home with the breath crashing in her ears. The speed camera down the bottom of her street flashes, stabbing-bright, but she doesn't slow down. Fingers numb around the steering wheel.

When she arrives, it's on the doorstep, looking up at her with the offended dignity of a cat whose feeding-time has been missed.

It perches on her shoulder as she eats dinner, as she reads her book with the burble of Darren's video game in the background. When she goes to bed, it follows.

It doesn't eat or drink. Doesn't seem to need anything but Myra's presence, whether it's riding her shoulder or hanging on around her neck or sitting in her lap. It's quiet, mostly. Her colleagues don't notice it. When Myra pops to her mum's for a cuppa after work, she cocks her head like she's trying to figure out what's different, but all she says is, "Is that a new coat, love?"

"You were with me when I bought it."

Mum shakes her head. "I swear my memory's getting worse." The creature plops itself down in Myra's arms once she's hung her coat up, demanding to be held. Her mum turns to put the kettle on. "Get some cups out, will you?"

The cupboard's full of mismatched mugs, stacked three high though Mum never has more than a couple of people over at a time. There's a bright red one, shaped like a strawberry—Myra's favourite when she was a kid. Today, the red seems muted and muddy. Myra draws her fingertip around the rim.

"Did you put this in the dishwasher?" she says. "You know you're not supposed to."

Mum looks vaguely at the mug. "I don't think so. You're the only one who ever drinks out of that kiddie mug, you know."

Myra turns it over between her hands. "Oh."

It's not only the mug. Walking home, with the creature curled around her neck, the lights leading into town seem fainter, as though she's seeing them through murky water.

When she reaches the flat, Darren's watching TV in the living room with the lights turned down low. Myra fiddles with the brightness, turning it up as far as it will go, but the room doesn't seem to get any lighter.

"Stop fiddling with that," Darren complains, "you're giving me a headache."

Myra pokes uselessly at the knob. "I think it's busted."

He peels himself out of his chair and comes over to peer in her eyes. "D'you need to go to the optician?" he says. "'S like Blackpool Illuminations in here." The creature looks up his nose in fascination as he touches Myra's cheek. "And you've got red all on your face. Must be allergic to something."

She pulls away from his touch and goes to check herself out in the bathroom mirror. Finds a patch of scaly, rubbed-sore skin on her right cheekbone, where the creature likes to nestle against her, on her pillow, at night.

Evidence. And Darren saw it.

It's real.

Darren hovers behind her in the bathroom doorway.

"You see this?" she demands.

"Well, yeah. Not being funny or anything, I just think you wanna put something on it. Looks sore."

Myra waves him away. "That means it's real. *This* is real." She grabs the creature's hand; it makes a startled noise, and she realises this is the first time she's touched it of her own volition. Maybe, before, she was afraid to have it confirmed she wasn't seeing things. "But you can't see it."

Darren shrugs helplessly. "See *what*, My?" There's an edge of exasperation in his voice. Myra sees him pull it back and force himself to soften. "I'm getting worried. Maybe you ought to go to the doctor."

She deflates and lets the creature's hand fall. "Where's the Sudocrem?" It coos and strokes her hair.

When she tries talking to Mum about it, Mum only purses her lips. "I thought you'd grown out of this."

"Out of what?" Myra tugs at the sleeves of her cardigan, tucking her hands up inside. The fabric has started to wear thin where her thumbs poke at the cuffs. Mum's mouth pinches tighter. Myra remembers being scolded for it as a teenager in a band hoodie and forces herself to stop.

"You know what, My." Mum sighs. "You mean well. But you get carried away."

Nice euphemism for *I think you're full of it*. "I'm not making this up."

"I know you don't think you are." Mum heaves herself to her feet; lays her hand on Myra's head as she passes.

Her hand brushes one of the creature's veiny ears, which twitches with interest. It turns its head to inspect her fingers. The beds of her nails look grey and faded, the colour of old ham. Its face is flushed—pinker than when it first appeared—and its eyes are bright.

Myra sighs and gets up to help with the dishes. She doesn't bring it up again.

Saturday. She's supposed to meet friends from her old job for lunch in Cardiff. She considers making an excuse, but the idea of sitting around the flat all day, with Darren seesawing between concern and impatience, and with the creature, makes her grind her teeth. By the time she leaves to catch the train, the ache in her jaw extends right down one side of her neck.

Her friends greet her with hugs like nothing's different, like it isn't right there, squished between them, as they kiss her cheek. She caked on foundation over the raw patch of skin this morning, lumpy and imperfect. Krissie eyes it as they sit but doesn't say anything.

Myra hasn't decided whether she's going to try and talk about the creature. She considers pretending everything's fine, even as it plays with her hair and sticks its fingers in her soup, but it's hard to focus on the conversation. Krissie's upcoming wedding, and what kind of bridesmaid dresses would suit them all. Myra's eyes fix on the grease stains the creature's fingers have left on the white tablecloth, and when Gemma asks her a question about necklines, she can only blink mistily in response. The photographs of dresses on Krissie's phone all look the same, colours faded like old film.

"I'm just saying," Gemma repeats, "I can't be walking around with my boobs out like it's Friday night on Mary Street, you know?"

"Oh my God, shut up about your boobs, there's grannies in here," Krissie hisses, looking to Myra as if for support. The creature tucks its head under Myra's chin, coarse fur scratching at her throat.

"My?" Gemma sets down her fork. "You okay? Look like you're miles away."

Myra rubs her forehead. The creature makes a creaky, protesting noise at being jostled. She's very tired, suddenly.

"It's just… has anything weird every happened to you? Like, you saw something, and it was real and you could touch it and it was *right there*, but you knew if you said anything to anyone they wouldn't believe you?"

Gemma nods solemnly. "I went to Spooky Sally in Aber last year. I know Krissie thinks it's a load of rubbish, but some of the stuff she knew about my nan…" She breathes out through her teeth.

Myra presses her eyes shut. Opens them. "No, nothing like that. There's this *thing*, and it's, it's always with me, and no-one can see it. Even you can't! Not even now!" Gemma peers at her. She gestures in front of her chest. "It's *right here*."

Krissie's expression clears. Her voice is softer—careful, like she's addressing a forgetful old relative or a sensitive child. "In your heart, you mean? My, if you're getting depressed again, you know you can always talk to us, right?"

Gemma nods in concert with her. "She's right. We're always here for you."

Myra drops her face into her hands. The creature pokes at her eyebrow.

She stops trying to talk about it. It's still there, though, growing more alive as the world around her greys. Though it doesn't change physically, Myra feels as though it's growing. Becoming weightier, expanding until it occupies every waking thought.

She's distracted all the time. Mum's sighs get more frequent, until Myra can hardly bear to visit her; invitations from Krissie and Gemma dry up. At work, she misses an important email and gets called into Susan's office for a bollocking. She tries to look contrite and attentive, she really does, but the creature keeps tugging at her ponytail and chewing on the collar of her blouse. When it stops, a string of drool hangs there, the bottom end leaving a damp spot on her chest. Susan's voice fades to a meaningless burble as Myra tries to figure out how she can discreetly wipe it away.

Susan clears her throat. "Am I boring you?"

Myra makes eye contact, aiming for sincere but, judging by the way Susan's brow furrows, lands on weirdly intense instead. "Sorry," she says. "Bit under the weather."

Susan huffs through her nose. "You shouldn't come in if you're feeling ill."

Myra remembers the last time she phoned in sick ("Are you *sure* you can't make it? A migraine's just a headache, isn't it?") and says nothing.

Darren looks at her like she might lose her rag at any little thing, these days. It sets her teeth on edge, makes her resentful. *He*'s always been the one with the temper. But she can't summon up the energy to give him an earful, either. She never has a moment to gather her thoughts in solitude, to put them in order, with the creature always hanging around her neck and making little half-speech, half-animal noises in her ear.

Sometimes she imagines one of them is a word, but when she studies its face for a flicker of comprehension, something human, it only regards her with animal blankness.

She and Darren move around each other in the flat, barely touching. Conversations never go beyond, "What do you want for tea?" or "Can you pick up toilet roll on your way home?" At night, the creature nestles on the pillow between them, always touching Myra. Any touch that might linger, she rolls away from, feigning sleep. Its presence is as prohibitive as that of a pet or a child.

She's not exactly surprised when Darren says, "I think I should move out." She feels outraged in a distant kind of way, like she might about an atrocity reported on the BBC or an acquaintance's marital woes. It doesn't hurt the way she thinks it should. It's just another itch, just another tug on her hair or waft of breath against her cheek.

The world gets a shade greyer.

She stays home most nights, keeps to herself at work. Eats at the kitchen table with the creature staring at her. Whatever she cooks is unappetising, like rubber in the mouth, and she can't even follow the plot of a TV programme. Ends up sitting in front of mindless DIY shows, watching participants coo over their new living rooms and feeling like she's sitting in a cell block.

The posters over the couch were mostly Darren's. She doesn't bother to replace them. Blobs of Blu-Tak cling to the wallpaper like old gum.

At first, she gets drunk a lot, wakes with her mouth wine-sour and calls in sick to work. She downloads music—albums she owned on CD as a teenager and thought she'd long outgrown—and cranks up the volume. Slipknot, My Ruin, System of a Down. The TV judders on its Wayfair cabinet and the upstairs neighbours bang on the ceiling, but she can still feel the creature's clutching fingers on her arms.

When she starts talking to it, it feels like the only thing she can do. That or silence, and on balance, the first makes her feel less insane.

She cajoles it. *Where's your home? Where'd you come from? There must be others like you, somewhere. Wouldn't you be happier with them?*

What about that woman you were with the first time I saw you?

It makes a snuffling noise and clings to her harder.

She yells at it.

I hate you, I hate you, I hate you. I never asked for this. Never wanted a kid or a puppy, never mind whatever you *are. Get away from me.*

Flecks of spit fly from her mouth. It cuddles closer, flat black eyes unblinking.

She tries to hurt it. Pummels it with her fists. Its flesh is springy and resilient, like a foam stress ball, and she doesn't leave a mark.

She throws it across the room with all her strength. It hits the wall and slides to the floor in a heap, the impact knocking over an empty bottle on the bookcase. After a few seconds, it gathers itself and waddles back over to her.

She goes at its face with the nail scissors. Rust-red blood gets under her fingernails and into the grooves of her knuckles. The cut gapes, ragged. By morning it has healed to an uneven, accusing pucker, and it perches on her shoulder in the shower as she scrubs her hands.

Myra mostly keeps to herself, these days; but one Saturday morning she realises she has no food for the weekend, and not enough money in her account to get a takeaway. Things have been tight since Darren moved out.

The thought of going outside makes her feel leaden, like an arthritic old woman trying to heave herself upright, but she puts on her coat and shoulders her handbag. The creature settles around her neck like a fur stole.

In town, Myra keeps her head down. Walks with purpose and doesn't look up when she hears what might be someone calling her name. If that's what it is, they don't call again. She buys oven chips, chicken fillets, some peas for vitamins. Mum always said you had to have something green on the plate. These days, it's easier to remember Mum as the all-knowing figure from her childhood, leaning over the table with serving spoon in one hand and the other planted on her hip, than to call her up and try to have a conversation.

A man across the street stares at her. He's alone, sixtyish, with thick glasses and a Jack Russell on a lead. Myra tries to retract her head into her winter coat like a turtle. No matter how normal she thinks she's acting, people look at her strangely. Like they can sense the creature even when they can't see it, like it is a mark placed on her telling them she no longer belongs.

The man keeps staring. Myra realises he's not looking at her. He's looking at the creature.

The man puts his head down and hurries off, tugging the dog behind him. Myra thinks of the woman at Tesco.

Could she do that? Hand it off to someone else and make a run for it? Be free?

A wave of self-revulsion runs through her. Put someone else through this? She turns on her heel and walks fast in the opposite direction to the man with the dog.

But the thought lingers. Itches.

A few weeks later, Susan calls her into the office again.

Myra's shoulders tighten as she leaves her desk, a now-familiar burning ache drawing her posture bow-tight. The creaure's weight is starting to make her hunch.

She knows what this is. She's had three disciplinaries already, and last week she somehow managed to delete the files for a big project that's due in a few days from the office servers. It took hours of overtime to get everything back. She's so tired lately, her thoughts thin and insubstantial and fading like vapour. The world scrubbed of colour, wasted down to a dream. The only thing that feels real is the creature.

Even Susan's mouth moving, as she says, "Not working out" and, "Going to have to let you go," feels like something watched on a projector screen: the image speckled with shadow, the sound a half-beat out of sync. Myra's hands, folded in her lap, seem detached from her, etiolated fish-belly white. They move of their own accord as she lets herself out of the office, gathers handbag and coat, and leaves. Once, Myra thinks, she'd at least have given Susan the finger.

She can't settle to the task of applying for new jobs. The woman in the Jobcentre sighs through Myra's explanations and looks askance at her when her eyes dart to the creature. She knows these places are designed to keep you small, and leaves feeling diminished anyway. The bright green sign out front looks the colour of mould.

A young woman, maybe twenty, sits smoking on the wall in front of the building. Her dirty blonde hair is scraped back from her narrow face with its pointy nose and sprinkling of acne on the chin. She scrolls through her phone, pausing for a cursory glance up as Myra walks out.

Then she freezes. Her eyes have found the creature.

The pulse fills Myra's throat and thumps there like a blender with a lump of something solid inside. *No, I couldn't*, she tells herself, and for a moment believes it, and then she is walking up to the girl.

The creature unfurls from its position on her shoulder, crooning curiously.

"Can you see it?" Myra demands. Her voice feels hoarse and unused, despite the fact she spent fifteen minutes pleading with the Jobcentre woman.

The girl blows out smoke and nods mutely. Her eyes are pale, watery blue, the right one crusted with sleep at its inner corner. A small part of Myra wants to wipe it away and buy her nicotine gum.

The creature extends a hand toward the girl. Her gaze fixes on it, and the fingers holding the cigarette tremble. Myra hardens.

She lifts the creature from her shoulder and, for once, it goes willingly, no talons snagging on her clothes, no fingers in her hair.

The girl's mouth works. "What the—"

Myra drops it in the girl's lap and runs.

Afterwards, she waits for colour to come back to the world.

She can't bear to stay cooped up in the flat after so many weeks alone with the creature, so she heads outside and walks for miles every day. Around the park and the town centre, and up into the hills where the grass is wet with dew and sprinkled with sheepshit.

Myra tries to recall what things looked like, before. Remembers yolk-yellow daffodils in the park, little boats on the pond in playschool primary colours, and the bright white feathers of the geese that hung around waiting for crisps and bits of bread. She remembers the shopfront signs in town—Superdrug pink and M&S green and Spar red—and the lit-up adverts in their windows and the blue-white-orange stripes on the buses. She even thinks longingly of the crushed green of trodden-down grass and the red-brown scars of exposed earth and the gold of a discarded Strongbow can winking in the bushes.

Myra goes further every day, like if she can get far enough from home, things might burst into glorious Technicolor all around her. *Welcome, Dorothy, you always knew Kansas wasn't the real world, didn't you?*

Sepia tones everywhere. The brief, bright flare of hope she felt when she handed the creature over turns corrosive, burning in her lungs when she gets breathless from walking. But she walks anyway, because what else is she going to do?

It's been maybe a month—her savings dwindling, Mum's worry nagging in the back of her head every moment—when Myra spots a familiar figure sitting in a doorway. The person's legs are splayed out in front of her, eyes fixed sightlessly on a blank spot of wall across the street. For a moment, Myra isn't sure why she recognises her.

The stranger turns her head, eyes fixing on Myra's face. A flash of some unidentifiable emotion before she looks quickly away.

She's wearing a raincoat. The colour is muddy, but Myra thinks it's British racing green.

Something stirs in the shadows of the doorway beside her. Myra tries to tell herself it's a rat.

The creature emerges slowly, with a noise like a cat's chirrup. It isn't the same grey-pink colour as Myra's creature—the fur darker, the face a deeper grey. A little bigger, too, Myra thinks.

It crawls up the woman's anorak. There are worn spots in the fabric that match its claws. When it reaches her shoulder, it settles there, one small arm slung across her throat. Her eyes glaze over. After a moment, she reaches up to pet its grey snout.

***JL George** lives in Cardiff and writes weird and speculative fiction. Her work has appeared in Fireside, Cossmass Infinities, Curiosities, and various other magazines and anthologies, and her first novel The Word is out now. In her other lives, she's a library-monkey and an academic interested in literature and science and the Gothic.*

The Obscurists

M Luke McDonnell

Taran had a bad reaction to portal travel, which is why Sierra always arrived first. He didn't barf or pass out–he seemed to have an actual physical allergy to the technology. He sneezed, broke out in hives, and had trouble breathing. Taking a pill before leaving didn't help. Sierra carried an EpiPen just in case, but so far caffeine and an antihistamine had always gotten him over the worst of it.

Sierra stepped through, shifting latitude and longitude from San Diego, California to Wheeling, West Virginia. For her, the passage felt like expecting one more tread on a staircase, discovering it wasn't there, and stepping down too hard and abruptly. The scent of salt air and coconut sunscreen was replaced by stale sweat, burnt popcorn, and disinfectant.

Wheeling's portal station appeared to be located in an until-recently-abandoned bus terminal. They'd plunked the thing down right in the middle of the room, pushed aside dusty banks of orange plastic chairs and used those to form barriers around the machine. Not an inappropriate location, come to think of it. The portals were the Greyhound buses of this era–cheap travel to nearly anywhere, although thankfully much faster.

Sierra now saw why it had taken days to get an arrival slot. There was only the one portal. A line of travelers waiting to depart zig-zagged across the stained linoleum floor and out the front door. The ragged family readying to go through had what appeared to be all their earthly possessions with them, packed into cardboard boxes, plastic bins, and suitcases held together with rope. Although the federal government was underwriting the cost of this modern highway system–San Diego had 50 each for arrivals and departures–the manufacturing and testing process was slow, and the big hubs got the machines first. Places like Wheeling were at the bottom of the list.

Sierra moved aside, pulled the Faraday tape from her pack, and wound it hurriedly round her wrist. Five layers should do it, but she added a few more, just to be safe.

A moment later, Taran stumbled from the portal, his summer-in-Seattle pale skin flushing pink in the humid West Virginia air.

"You okay?" She led him to a dusty bench away from the crowd, pulled the "Taran survival pack" from her bag, and handed him a Benadryl and a Zazz Cola.

Taran popped the pill and took deep, wheezy gulps of the soda.

"I'm okay," he said, although he leaned his head against the wall and shut his eyes.

Sierra ripped half a meter of silver tape from the roll and wrapped it around the damp skin of his left wrist. Faraday tape wasn't meant to be used this way. It wasn't toxic, but the adhesive was too strong, as evidenced by the lack of hair on Taran's lower arm. She took the detector from her pocket, waved it over his wrist and her own and didn't get so much as a beep. Excellent. Painful as it was to remove, the tape was the best way to keep their embedded screens from sending and receiving signals. If a network discovered she was here, their competitors could as well.

Taran leaned forward, his skin returning to a less-alarming shade of pink. "Let's get a move on. I don't want to lose our head start."

Sierra glanced at the portal. "You think Logan and Vance know about this place?"

"Of course. They get the same bulletins we do, but 57 new portals opened in the last week and there's no reason they'd choose to come here. Everyone's headed to Antarctica this weekend, that's what I hear. Granted, obscurists don't generally show their hands, so who knows."

Sierra hated Logan and Vance, and hate wasn't too strong a word. The non-identical twins, former child stars, came late to the game of finding forgotten, obscure-but-significant places and geo-tagging them. Sierra and her friends had been doing it for over a year, building the community and the rules, then Logan and Vance blew it all up. Now every teen with a few credits was jumping through portals hoping to tag something they'd found in their parent's rotting encyclopedias and trying to land a spot on Logan and Vance's hit streamcast.

"They followed us to the Big Island last weekend," Sierra said.

"We don't know that."

"Three minutes after we found the King Kamehameha statue in the lava tube they were there. You think that was a coincidence? We barely registered our claim before they jammed our signal. That's against the code!"

Taran shrugged. "We're in the top 10 and they aren't, not even with all their sponsors and fancy equipment. Don't get distracted by them. We're better at this and we'll get another tag today if we get moving." He unrolled a poster-sized printout of his latest prize, a 1920s map of

Wheeling. "We need to head south on Market Street, east on 15th, then into to the woods, assuming the property isn't fenced off."

Sierra hoped it was. Her bag held lock picks, bolt cutters, a hacksaw, and the latest electronic lock brain-frying device. Chances are she wouldn't need any of it. Fences in places like this were more signifiers than barriers. Strange that people who owned rural property were so casual about securing it. She'd always lived in rented apartments, and although they weren't technically hers, there was no way she'd let someone traipse through her patio. It might only be a 4x8 piece of concrete but she'd installed lasers and a motion-activated sprinkler system that kept raccoons and possibly thieves away.

Taran, who'd been eager to leave, was now absorbed in the map, tracing thin lines with his finger and muttering.

"You wanted to get going?" Love of ancient data was his strength and weakness.

"Yes." He answered a few seconds after he should have, then rolled the map with practiced ease and put it back in the tube. "Onwards!"

He was too thin to be much of a human shield, but she sidled behind him as he wormed his way through the crowd and out of the station.

The mob of residents waiting to depart clogged the cracked sidewalk that hugged the side of the old bus station. Sierra expected quizzical looks as they made their way south against the flow. Wheeling wasn't a tourist town and the portal had been in place less than a week. A few children noticed her cameaux jacket changing to match the surroundings and whispered to each other, but the adults leaned into the scant shade of the brick wall and focused on a place other than where they were.

"They don't get it," Sierra whispered when she and Taran were out of earshot. "They don't have to move. They can keep their cheap rents here and work anywhere."

"You don't know what it's like to feel trapped," Taran said. "They're seeing a door marked 'Exit' and they're worried it might disappear next week. A lot has been taken from this community. For all they know, the portal might be next. This city was a major terminus of the B&O railway line in the 1800s, and the busiest in the state. Once the city ran out of coal, the world built a bypass around them."

Taran was getting his PhD at the University of Washington, and Sierra was never sure if it was his thesis research or fascination with defunct railroads talking. There seemed to be quite a big overlap so it probably didn't matter. She was lucky to have him as a partner. He'd picked her from the thousands on the forum because of her record number of arrests for trespassing. He might be amazing at finding places lost in time, but he was terrible at breaking rules.

The downtown's charming but vacant storefronts gave way to the genteel poverty of Victorian mansions in disrepair, and after a few more blocks, less photogenic decay: two-story tall, flat-faced brick buildings with blackened upper-floor eye sockets, mouth front doors gaping open, mobile homes with blue tarps for roofs and "No Tresspassing" sprayed on the moldy vinyl siding.

"By next week, Wheeling will be overrun and property values will have doubled," Taran said. "The residential areas need some TLC, but this place is a time capsule. Real estate agents love that. Did you see the old theater?"

Sierra gave up on the sidewalk after the fifth pile of trash bags and walked in the street. "I did. A mime troupe from Brooklyn will be performing there next Saturday."

Taran stopped. "Really? It's already sold?"

She swatted his shoulder and he nearly tripped over an abandoned rocking chair. "No! I'm kidding. Kidding not kidding I guess, if you're right. And you're always right. We've been first in to so many about-to-be-interesting places, thanks to you. I've got a good feeling about today."

Taran waved the detector and it played a discordant symphony.

"That's just the locals tagging," Sierra said, consulting her own detector. "We're the first real hunters."

15th Street dead-ended into the suggestion of a fence–a single strand of barbed wire strung between two bleached wooden posts. Taran skirted this without his usual hesitation and headed down a crooked dirt trail that picked up where the road stopped.

"The tracks were pulled up in the 1960s, but this is where the spur of the B&O railroad would have been that led to the Little Creek coal mine. Look." He reached into the grass and pulled out a rusty spike. "We're on the right track."

"Ha ha."

"I wasn't joking."

"I know. You aren't much of a joker."

The morning sun inched toward noon and the heat and humidity intensified. Sierra was soon as damp as if she'd run through sprinklers. Still, she'd take this over the dryness of the Andes. Her chapped lips from that trip had only just healed.

After they'd traversed an overgrown field and made it to the fringes of a forest, Taran paused, looked furtively left and right, then pulled another map from his pack, this one folded origami-neat. The hand-drawn ink lines, cross-hatching, flourishes, and square serif fonts suggested it was from the late 1800s. Sierra wasn't sure when she'd assimilated Taran's vintage cartography knowledge, but now she could read documents like this as easily as a metro map.

He lowered his voice, though the only creature besides Sierra that could hear him was a distantly barking dog. "I didn't want to tell you what we were after until we were actually here. I don't buy your theory that our private messages have been hacked or that other hunters can track us, but–"

She held up her silver-swathed wrist. "They have been and they can. You find places that are utterly lost, on maps that aren't digitized, in archives that aren't available to the general public. If anyone shows up here, it's because we've been followed."

She suspected that for Taran, the real hunt happened in the special collections rooms of the libraries he visited. Hunting and tagging was more to confirm the artifacts existed than for the thrill of ownership Sierra felt when she tagged and claimed one of the ever-diminishing number of forgotten places on the planet.

"We're looking for a tunnel," his voice a low whisper. "Not just any tunnel. A tunnel that is very probably the one featured in Mark Twain's famous story, 'A Coal Black Night.'"

She wanted to mirror his excitement, but couldn't. "I've only read the one about the frogs." Taran knew she read science fiction when she read at all.

He gave up whispering. "It was very well known, at the time. A couple of tramps spend the night in a tunnel and see a ghost."

Sierra shook her head.

"Mark Twain passed through this area six months before the story was published, and the tunnel was described in great detail. If we can prove this is the setting, we'll be cited in journals."

Taran loved being cited. She didn't mind either, though her friends weren't particularly impressed when she ended up in places like the *Missouri Historical Review*.

Taran poked a dashed line. "The tracks skirted a farm, but we can head straight north from here and catch up with them again once we cross the creek. That'll save us a lot of walking. From there, the tunnel should be just another kilometer."

"Why hasn't anyone claimed it yet? It's so close to a town."

"First, no portal until now, and second, very few people know about it. The spur was never used. The company went bankrupt before the mine opened and the tracks were never mapped."

Sierra did her best to raise one eyebrow but despite practice, failed.

He got the point. "This isn't a railroad map. It's a survey of the farm. The tracks defined the eastern edge of the property. The surveyor got curious, so he went to see where they led and marked the tunnel. I've not seen any reference to it anywhere else."

"Well, let's go claim it."

She'd only taken a few steps off the path when Taran grabbed her arm.

"Careful," he said, pointing to a low, green bush. "That's poison ivy. Causes a bad rash. We don't have it on the west coast."

Sierra examined the innocuous green leaves. It was hard to differentiate them from the rest of the vegetation. "You aren't allergic, I hope."

"No," Taran said. "Thankfully."

Thankfully indeed, given he was standing in it.

They tromped through the woods without speaking after that. That's how it usually went–a flurry of activity upon arrival, then they settled into wherever they'd landed.

The barking of the distant dog faded, replaced by birdsong. Sierra had to stop herself from whistling along. Most locations they visited weren't this pleasant. The ground was level and softly carpeted with the remnants of last year's fallen leaves. Each slender-trunked tree stood a respectful distance from its neighbor and the canopy cut the heat of the early summer sun. Peaceful places like this were rare in an overcrowded world. City people wanting to get the most out of a nature weekend went for drama–Yosemite, Big Sur, Death Valley. Getting away from it all meant standing shoulder to shoulder with Leah from Los Angeles and Nate from New York, both of them complaining about the terrible service they'd gotten in the pizzeria last night.

The quiet perfection of an old-growth forest was exactly what Sierra needed after a tough week at work. Her first real job after graduation paid well, but the engineers she worked with wouldn't yield a centimeter of territory to the "new hire," and she ended up on all the shit projects.

Taran shuffled ahead, an old-fashioned compass held in front of him like a divining rod. Ten minutes later, the promised creek appeared. He stepped carefully across using flat stones as a bridge; Sierra bounded it in a leap, almost but not quite keeping her boots dry.

The forest gave way to a bright meadow. Taran walked a few meters into it–and fell to his knees. Sierra worried he'd twisted his ankle until she caught up and saw him caressing thin, rusted rails that wove through the tall grass and sky blue wildflowers.

"They're here. They weren't pulled up." He beamed. "This is the first time I've been glad my sources were wrong."

Sierra shaded her eyes and followed the tracks north. "There's a house over there."

An ancient, single-story red brick structure abutted the tracks. The thin, arched windows were covered with plywood and the intricately-carved wooden door in colorful graffiti. The slate-tiled roof was mostly intact, the exception being the nearest corner, where an intrepid tree burst through. Morning glories spilled from the rain gutters and swayed in the faint breeze.

Taran hurried toward the place, compass waving wildly. "This is in the story! It shouldn't be here. No one builds a train station in the middle of a spur. I thought it was a Mark Twain exaggeration." He put a foot on steps to what Sierra had thought was a deck but now realized was a platform. The wood groaned.

"Leave that be," she said. "I see the tunnel." The wavering tracks led to a black blot in the viridian foliage.

Taran wheeled, took a step, then froze and stared down.

"I don't care if you found the magical golden spike that's in the story, we need to tag this." Sierra, sweaty again now that she was back in the beating sun, tromped through the grass toward him. He didn't move. Instead, he sat on the edge of a railroad tie and rolled up the fabric of his right pant leg. A tiny red spot on his ankle bloomed to a bulls-eye as Sierra watched.

"What happened?"

"I think I was stung by a bee." He plucked a small black speck from the center of the growing welt.

"You're allergic," Sierra said, recognizing the symptoms.

"Very. It's okay, I've got the pen." He was oddly calm, the way he was when he studied maps.

The red spread up his ankle as he fumbled in his bag. "I've never actually had to use it," he said, a wheeze in his voice. "Do you think you could inject me? I'm not a big fan of needles."

"Of course you're not." She'd bandaged his cuts countless times and he'd always found a logical reason to look away. A needle would be easy. She could do this.

Taran gave up fumbling and upended the bag. Maps, a flashlight, a half-eaten chocolate bar, a bottle of water, a comb, a notepad–and no EpiPen.

He dropped the bag, leaned to the side, and threw up.

"Sorry," he croaked. The veins on his face and neck pulsed.

"Don't worry," Sierra said. "I've got a pen as well."

It was in the purple satchel she brought on every trip. Zazz Cola. Benadryl. Epinephrine inhaler. EpiPen. The Taran survival pack. She fumbled for the pen, relieved when her hand closed around the plastic-wrapped cylinder.

Something wasn't right. The pen was too heavy, and her thumb ran back and forth across three bumps that shouldn't be there. She pulled it out. The tamper-evident seal of the original packaging leaked red.

She ripped open the plastic. What lay in her palm wasn't from a pharmacy but an R&D lab. Status lights. Antenna. Lens. Microphone. A state-of-the-art tracking device? Who could afford something like this? Two overpaid streamcast stars, that's who.

"What the hell."

Taran retched.

She dropped the thing onto the tracks and stomped it with her all-terrain boot. The lights went out and the case cracked but it didn't bust into a million pieces like she'd hoped.

Taran collapsed into the weeds–eyes shut, face swollen, honeybees dangerously close. "Go tag the tunnel," he whispered.

"No fucking way." She worked to pry the tape off her wrist. The heat had melted the glue to an even more adhesive state. She clawed a few centimeters free, gripped the loose end with her teeth, and painstakingly unraveled the rest. Why had she used a meter of this when half would have worked just as well?

The last bit came free with a snap.

Her position was now available to anyone and everyone.

"911," She yelled when the screen lit up. "I need an EpiPen. Taran Ramirez 9002753863926 is here and has been stung by a bee."

Even middle-of-nowhere places had drone paramedics. She'd memorized Taran's ID last year after he'd bet her a beer she couldn't do it after only seeing it once. She'd won. The numbers played a song in her head. She hummed it now although she, too, felt sick.

"They'll find us," Taran croaked, and he wasn't referring to the flying doctors.

"They will, but don't worry. Next weekend we'll tag something better." Sierra tried to keep her tone light as Taran faded from red to ghostly white. She rolled up her bag and put it under his head, then spoke softly to her wrist. Severe bee sting allergy. The pixels said he could die. He couldn't. He hadn't finished his thesis. People didn't die like this. It wasn't possible.

Minutes later, the whine of a drone cut through the birdsong and Sierra let out a breath she hadn't realized she'd been holding.

The drone that appeared wasn't a medic, but an eight-bladed monstrosity with a pendulous, 360-degree VR globe camera swinging beneath it.

Logan and Vance smashed their way through the woods moments later, decked out in matching FlyTyme gear. Their sponsor wished they were identical twins and styled them as such. Sierra hated their matching hairstyles, the tattoos that began on one and ended on the other, and their fucking perfect teeth.

Logan flashed a peace sign as he jogged by.

"Where's my EpiPen?" Sierra yelled. "I need it!"

"No idea what that is, sweetheart."

"It's about the size and shape of a tracking device, but it's full of medicine."

Logan lowered his forefinger and the peace sign now told her to fuck off. "You're trying to distract me, and I'm not falling for it. Remember the hot springs?"

She did. She and Taran were close to tagging a hot spring in Guatemala–once thought to be a fountain of youth–when they'd heard Logan and Vance and their entourage tramping up the mountain trail in the forest behind them. They might have a big budget but they had zero stealth. Sierra ran back a few dozen meters and repositioned the arrow on an old wooden sign directing hikers. It was a cartoonish ruse that shouldn't have worked, but it had. In their haste, the twins ignored their GPSs and ran up the wrong path. She'd gotten the tag, and that might have been the end of it, but she'd bragged about what she'd done on the forum, and the twins were mocked. Since then, the twins had dropped any pretense of friendly rivalry and had become downright nasty–and the game a lot less fun.

Today it wasn't a game at all. Sierra cradled Taran's head in her lap and tried to figure out if she had what she needed for an emergency tracheotomy or whatever the fuck she would have to do to keep him breathing.

The next whir, which she'd worried was a swarm of bees, was the paramedic drone.

The pearlescent ovoid was an amazingly efficient machine, scanning Taran's wrist–now tape-free–drawing blood, and administering an antidote all in less than 60 seconds.

Taran began to breathe easier almost immediately. Five minutes later he sat up and drank the water Sierra offered.

Given your medical history, you should never travel without an EpiPen the drone admonished on its pixilated screen.

"We know," Sierra said. "It was an accident. Thank you for your help." She felt a bit faint herself and wondered if she should ask for aid, but she figured if she ate the rest of Taran's rapidly melting chocolate bar she'd be okay.

The drone's screen displayed the amount due and Sierra held up her wrist. Taran tried to protest but she shut him up.

"I'll follow you to Seattle and you can buy me a beer. Let's rest for a minute before we head back." She helped him to the shade of the old station. "You feeling better?"

"I am."

The swelling on his ankle and face had subsided and he took full, deep breaths.

"Was that Logan and Vance?" he asked.

"It was."

"You were right. They've been tracking us. We lost the tunnel." He sagged against the stone foundation.

"But we didn't lose you." She held up her hand for a high five. He didn't reciprocate.

"I'm sorry. This was a big one. Really obscure with real history."

He hoisted himself up, one hand on her shoulder and one on a stone that jutted from the foundation, and stood, staring at the old station.

Sierra didn't object when he tried the stairs to the platform again. There was a chance they'd break, but she wanted him away from the flowers and the bees.

The stairs complained but didn't collapse. Taran rubbed at a piece of plastic nailed to the front door, then stared at it for so long Sierra gave up and risked the stairs to join him. The text on the old sign read "For Sale," and his rubbing had revealed a QR code–a geometric pattern of squares popular in advertisements 50 years ago.

He held up his wrist to scan it, then paged through the text on his screen. "This place is still for sale. Twenty acres, which includes the station and," he couldn't contain a widening smile, "the tunnel."

Sierra didn't follow.

"Do you have 10,000 credits?" he asked. "I do. Between the two of us we can buy this place and use it as a home base for our weekend hunts. We can own history. Real history. Isn't that what we've been trying to do? Own something?"

Sierra swayed in the sun, trying to sort game from reality. She'd never owned anything she couldn't fit in the back of a small transport pod.

"We don't have much time," Taran said. "When Logan and Vance start broadcasting, prices will skyrocket."

She took a careful step back and gazed up at the building. Someone long ago had placed alternating red and white bricks above the arched windows and carved swallows into the eaves. Her plasticrete apartment building in San Diego looked like every other building on the block and when the Santa Ana winds blew, pieces of it flaked off and flew into the Pacific. This building had been standing for more than 200 years. Hers might last 20.

"What the hell. Let's do it." This time Taran reciprocated her high five.

A few taps and fingerprints later, the deed, literally, was done.

Taran jiggled the lock on the front door. "Can you pick this? I want to check out our new clubhouse."

"I can, but first..." She dialed 911 again. "Sheriff's Department please. I just spotted some intruders on my property."

She pulled a fat paint marker from her pack and wrote "No Tresspassers" on the front door.

She owned this.

***M. Luke McDonell's** work has appeared in Shoreline of Infinity, The Overcast, The Arcanist, Perihelion, New Reader Magazine, and more. Additionally, she produces the SF in SF podcast, a monthly author reading event.*

By day, she is a senior visual designer by night she writes and helps run SomaFM internet radio. Follow her on Twitter @Mlukemc and learn more at /mlukemcdonell.wordpress.com

Books

The Review Team

The Prestige

Christopher Priest

So, this isn't a new book, and it's not a new author. But it's an excellent one and if, like me, you missed it first time around you won't want to miss it twice. *The Prestige* won the World Fantasy Award, and the author is a multiple Hugo nominee and BSFA award winner. It's even been made into a film (a very good one, too, by all accounts). But its author, Christopher Priest, died earlier this year and it seemed fitting to review one of his novels, to reflect on the first rate writer that he was. Also, I'd never read this one and the chance to review it was a wonderful excuse to rescue it from the to-be-read pile.

And what an excellent book it is, too. It's gothic, which is a massive plus right from the start, and doesn't disappoint with its slow-build creepiness. Two Victorian stage magicians become bitter rivals, each trying to undermine the other by sabotaging their respective acts. Their accounts are shown, in true Victorian style, though a series of journal entries. These accounts are unreliable, of course (as admitted by one of the writers – they're magicians, after all), which add to the sense of instability that runs through this novel. No certainties here: how *do* they do these magic tricks?

Alfred Borden is working class: his great rival, Rupert Angier is the son of a Lord, but they both find their way in magic. Borden, outraged at what he perceives to be the charlatan tricks of seances performed by Angier exposes him as a fraud, and so the rivalry begins. Later, Borden perfects an impossible trick where he disappears and reappears elsewhere, almost simultaneously, as if teleporting. Angier is obsessed in learning the secret, but ends up with a trick (if it is a trick) far stranger, and far more disturbing, than anything his bitter adversary has conceived.

All this is wrapped in a present-day story of the two magicians' descendants searching for a way to reconcile the past. This framing device is suitably gothic too, but don't expect any of the answers you might expect.

The spookiness comes late in this novel, but there are hints of the supernatural throughout. And when it comes, it doesn't let up. This isn't a novel you should put down three-quarters read.

You end up not sympathising for any of these characters, though, apart from maybe the magicians' long-suffering wives (and their shared mistress). I felt sorry for them, though, wrapped up in their obsessions and their inadequate understandings of their worlds. This is a story of duality, of rivalry and of obsession. The results are not pretty. Recommended.

As for Christopher Priest's wider works, try any of his BSFA winning novels: 1974's *The Inverted World,* 1998's *The Extremes,* 2002s *The Separation* or 2011's *The Islanders.* His books are generally strange and unsettling but grounded and engaging and, like all great novels, tap into human nature with all its flaws. His long and prolific career culminated with 2023's *Airside,* though there is said to be another, unpublished novel (*The Cull*) which I am eagerly awaiting. In the meantime, there's the film version of *The Prestige* to track down: Hugh Jackman and Christian Bale in dimly-lit gothic malevolence. I can hardly wait.

Mark Bilsborough

The Ship

Antonia Honeywell

"I am living on a ship of my father's creation. I live with five hundred people whom my father has chosen." These are the opening words of this intriguing debut novel by Antonia Honeywell. The repetition of 'my father' being nicely indicative of the main thrust of the story.

Don't be put off by the cover if you purchase the same version as me – the soft orange and yellow hues and the silhouette of a figure on the prow of a ship could suggest a romance. And while there are explorations of love here, the theme is speculative, the genre post-apocalyptic.

The protagonist – Lalla – is 16 years old and "was born at the end of the world" in London. We instantly become part of an tough environment where all available food is tinned or dried; floods and fires are commonplace; Regent's Park is now a shanty town and in the British Museum, there are hundreds of homeless, hungry people living hand to mouth – potentially literally as cannibalism exists in parts of the world.

Lalla however, has it easier than most, as her father's job has enabled the family a better lifestyle than most. He has invented a system called 'Dove': an ID card scheme whereby everyone must register in order to be informed where to find food etc. However, the 'Dove' system is harsh, not helpful. Without an ID card you do not exist in the eyes of the Government. Without an ID card, you could be shot on sight.

Watching his invention disintegrate into a tool for devastation and deprivation inspires Michael to begin a new project. He begins to equip a huge ship, big enough to offer long term salvation for 500 people, secretly interviewed and chosen by him. Lalla's mother however, is not keen on this idea of abandoning so many needy people behind and is openly reluctant to leave.

When the ship finally embarks, it isn't without drama. And Lalla's life of privilege is painfully exposed when she cannot– and will not – connect or empathise with other people's stories of tragedy or loss. She shuts herself in her cabin and when she re-emerges, it is only to discover that her father has begun to style himself as *everyone's* father, soon becoming a Messiah type figure. The concept that her father dilutes his love for her at a time when she needs him the most is a springboard for many of the events that follow.

Lalla's character is strong, stubborn and often frustrating. However, the beauty of this novel is that we are very much a part of her growth and maturity. We are as shocked as she is when things are revealed as not being as they seem and we are rooting for her when she makes difficult decisions.

Described by Fiona Wilson in The Times as: "*The Hunger Games* meets the London riots on board Noah's Ark 20 years from now, The Ship is a dystopian story with a twist and a definite possibility of a sequel. Ignore the plot holes – how *did* Michael find all those supplies? – and enjoy.

Sandra Baker

Mercy of the Gods

James S.A. Corey

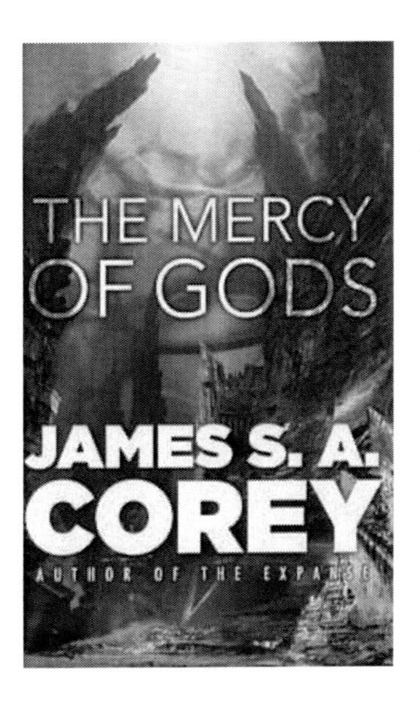

The latest from the creators of the *Expanse, The Mercy of the Gods* gives us new aliens, new threats and new, bemused, reluctant heroes. And, like the Expanse, it sets up a future conflict that suggests this is far from the last time we'll see its bowed but undefeated cast of enslaved scientists, waiting patiently to break the yoke of the oppressor Carryx.

This is a familiar type of space opera, but one that Daniel Abraham and Ty Franck (collectively James S.A. Corey) have a good track record of delivery in. The set up is a human colony (Anjiin) with a competing set of science teams who have just bridged the biological gap between humans and the alien species of the planet. But then the aliens arrive, kill one tenth of the population as a show of strength and capture the scientists, whisking them off to their home planet to replicate their experiments more widely – or die.

On the Carryx's planet they find many other species with the same mission and the mantra is be useful or die. Needless the humans find a way to do both…

The main protagonist, Dafyd Alkhor is a research assistant , but he soon grows in prominence and influence when his team is captured, becoming the main communications link with the aliens. The humans plan insurrection, but there is a bigger picture. Dafyd has the find a way to reconcile conflicting priorities and cope with some awful choices. Does he succeed? Well, there are a couple of sequels planned so you can probably guess how far along we are.

It's a slow start and it takes time to properly introduce the main characters – the main alien threat doesn't appear until a quarter of the way in (I was beginning to think the wrong blurb had been attached to the dust jacket) and when it does it's not subtle, though any action an invasion might make (resistance fighting etc) takes place off-camera and we stick with the scientists and their experiments. That's frustrating m because I wanted to know what was happening on Anjiin (or on any other human world, if there are any. This book is pretty much silent on that). We almost see the humans trying to go out in a blaze of glory, which would have been exciting, but the writers sidestep that. There's a tragic love affair, though its potential will, sadly, not see its way through to the sequels.

If I'm sounding ambivalent it's because I am. Its slow start aside, this has an *Expanse*-like pace and a plotline with possibilities. But there's nothing new here and the cast of characters is larger and less distinct than the tight-knit crew of the Rocianate (from the *Expanse*), which makes it harder to connect with them. That, together with some unsatisfying narrative choices, means the sequel isn't going to be on my Christmas wish list. Other reviews have been proudly positive, though, and this is an easy read so I suspect people pining for a post *Expanse* fix won't be wholly dissatisfied.

Mark Bilsborough

The Ministry of Time

Kaliane Bradley

Kaliane Bradley's energetic first novel, *The Ministry of Time* has attracted plenty of controversy already, and it's only just been released. Fans of foreign language SF may well be familiar with the Spanish TV series of the same name (*El Minsterio del Tempo)* and the producers were less than happy with what they saw as an opportunist rip-off, particularly as the BBC had jumped in with an audio version of Bradley's story. It mainly just shares the name, though, plus the central premise that there's a Government ministry with time travel capabilities reaching back to the past. That's probably enough for a lawsuit, but the two stories don't really share the same DNA. *El Minsterio del Tempo* is more like the TV series *Travellers* (they objected to that, too) and Bradley's book is really a culture clash romance with some interesting sci-fi twists.

The Ministry of Time never actually takes us into the past (or the future). Instead, having discovered time travel, a secret Government agency plucks a few people from various points in the past and sticks them in a safe house, overseen by Civil Servants. The people taken were all on the cusp of death, to avoid contamination of the timeline. The first-person narrator (who, irritatingly, isn't named) is Cambodian-English, learning to come to terms with her unusual cultural mix. Her job is to act as a 'bridge', to acclimatise an Arctic explorer from the 1840s into modern life. Commander Graham Gore had 'died', along with, ultimately, the rest of his crewmates, in 1847. He's based on a real character, and this novel shows some meticulous research into the period. Gore and his bridge inevitably become close but things begin to unravel when a visitor from the future start probing around.

Along the way this is an exploration of people from one culture thrust into a bewildering new world. Gore never quite gets to grips with the modern world, but finds his place, as does Arthur (gay, from WW1) and Margaret (gay, from the 1600s.), who relax into their new freedoms. Gore smokes a lot, acts inappropriately and eventually (re)joins the military, but he's also kind, charming and considerate.

Most of the novel concentrates on the steady build-up of understanding and affection between the narrator and Gore, but the last few chapters veer wight into sci-fi as the nature (and limitations) of the time travel project are revealed and the safe houses are compromised.

The prose is compelling and the characters are original and engaging, so it's easy to get swept along with this novel. That said, the set-up is unconvincing (relatively new, barely trained female Civil Servant given a crucial 'bridge' role in a super-secret project with a military man from a misogynist culture?) and the scope of the time travel project limited and underexplored. The purpose of the time-plucking was never really explained (unlike, say in the excellent *Extracted* by R.R. Haywood where heroes are sought to avert future catastrophe) and the tonal shift between the bulk of the book and the ending feels unnecessary. But this is a clever and seductive book which resists the temptation to do too much – I liked it.

Mark Bilsborough

Service Model

Adrian Tchaikovsky

One of best storytellers in the business', writes John Scalzi on the cover of Andrian Tchaikovsky's latest novel *Service Model,* and it's hard to argue. Of late, he's been giving us expansive space opera such as the excellent *Children of Time* series, but he's nothing if not versatile (eg his BSFA award fantasy novel *City of Last Chances*) and this, although still SF, is a delightful departure from his (albeit eclectic) norm.

It's light hearted post-apocalyptic tale, often bordering on comedy, but packing a serious punch. It's a future where the humans have all but disappeared and the robots – not quite intelligent enough for AI – are all behaving as though they're still serving their 'masters' until errors, glitches and contradictions caused by the complete breakdown of civilisation gets their little metal heads spinning leading to all sorts of irrational behaviour.

Charles is a valet in a mansion formerly inhabited by one of the rich humans with enough foresight to cut himself off from the rest of the disintegrating world. Except Charles has slit his master's throat when shaving him, so he's out of a job and feels compelled to find out why he should have deviated from his primary programming in such a gruesome fashion. He's not exactly self-aware, but he's getting there, thanks to a human called 'The Wonk' who Charles (now unCharles, because his name was tied to the job he no longer has) encounters and can't seem to get rid of, who seems intent into goading him into full self-determination. UnCharles, naturally, thinks the Wonk is a defective robot, which leads to some great comedic moments. Together they navigate a world where robots wait patiently in line until they rust to the spot, libraries that destroy everything in the process of protecting it, robot soldiers fighting endless, pointless wars and, ultimately 'god', or at least the AI equivalent.

UnCharles is a great point of view character. His search for work is a programming compulsion but he's not quite the unthinking automaton he keeps arguing (unconvincingly) that he is. The starting premise is that artificial life is inherently stupid, but as the novel progresses it's clear that how dumb the silly robots doing meaningless tasks ad infinitum are, the humans who programmed them are dumber still. The reasons for society's collapse are revealed in the final chapters, as the book gets all serious and message-y, but it's hardly a spoiler to say it all ended not with a bang but with a whimper. And in the end we find out why UnCharles was so slapdash with the cutthroat razor.

The author must have had great fun writing this one and it's certainly great fun to read. Unusual, quirky and surprisingly though-provoking, there's surely a grain of truth in amongst the exaggerated characters and seemingly ridiculous situations. It couldn't end like this, could it?

The Horses

Janina Matthewson

A post-apocalypse tale set on a remote (Scottish?) island, where a strange red mist has blanketed the mainland and cut off all communications. The hurried and unscheduled return of the island's ferry, with its cargo of dead and traumatised pilot raises questions with no easy answers. Isolated and fearful, the islanders return to self-sufficiency and life goes on. Attempts to reach the mainland fail, sometimes with tragic consequences, affecting the islanders in different ways.

Before the mist, young Sarah had her life's ambitions before her on the mainland. But now, trapped in the small confines of the bemused island community, she is forced to re-evaluate.

There are a couple of unsuccessful attempts to reach the mainland (which is normally accessible via a long peninsula as well as the ferry), but escape doesn't seem possible until horses return to the island, suggesting the red mist is dissipating and danger is receding. The horses, I guess, are a metaphor for freedom, resilience and vitality and they match the struggles of the islanders.

The islanders cope quite well, under the circumstances. It's a small, agricultural community with ample means to feed itself and, well used to a disconnected lifestyle, slips easily into new routines. Some islanders cope with the fear and isolation better than others, and this is in a way a story of survival and acceptance.

Everything is vague and non-specific: the location of the island, the nature of the crisis, the reason for the gradual rolling back of the mist. And there's a strong sense of powerlessness about the situation the islanders find themselves in, as if driven by forces of of their control. This, in a way, mirrors rural life, where nature is harnessed, temporarily, but every now and again with storms and snow and floods, we can only respond, never master.

The central relationship in the novel is between stay-at-home Ana and want-away Sarah, estranged but gradually reconciling. The book's more about relationships like these than it is about apocalypse (don't read this expecting *The Road*) and it's quietly effective – never demonstrative but always gently written with an eye for good characterisation.

The author, Janina Matthewson, is a New Zealander living in London and has a couple of other novels out, which I'll be tracking down (*Of Things Gone Astray* and *Just Below the Ribs* (co-authored with Jeffrey Croner). She also has a long running podcast: *Between the Wires*. Definitely worth checking out.

Mark Bilsborough

Manufactured by Amazon.ca
Acheson, AB